The Deadly Fruit of Original Si

The Deadly Fruit of Original Sin: A Psyc [illegible] asy, Ripper Tale.

Written and researched by John Lenard Stone

This book is a work of pure fantasy faction. Any similarities to persons living or dead, unless used fictitiously is pure coincidence.

All enquiries to;

John L Stone

Jhnstn87@aol.com.

In sincere respect of:

Sir. Frederick Treves, to whom I have nothing but admiration and respect, for his loyalty towards the Elephant Man and all people he served at the London Charity Hospital in Whitechapel.

And to Joseph Merrick, to whom I have nothing but empathy, for all the suffering at the hands of those cruel people who'd brought harm upon his poor soul.

And to all the women who'd died at the hands of Jack the Ripper. Their barbaric murders brought shame upon London.

And to Isaac Angel whose despair we could never envisage upon the unnatural murder of his wife and unborn child.

A special thanks.

For my darling wife Christine, to whom I dedicate this book.

Introduction.

Having a spiritual mind gives me at least one qualification to write a psychological fantasy faction narrative regarding my suspects in the hunt for Jack the Ripper and the people behind the deaths of the many women that worked the streets in the East End of London during the year of 1888. There are many aimless theories and suggestions surrounding Jack and his true identity, but my story is not just another Ripper yarn taboot, for it is a kaleidascope of circumstances that truly relies upon substance, since I have researched each murder with an open mind. And I have considered certain facts surrounding each case on its merits to draw my own conclusions. And as not to cause a stir among living relatives and sympathisers, I have written my tale as a psychological fantasy which equates to a fictitious account of what actually occurred back then. I have assiduously researched many high profile figures, sometimes in abject torment, just to find some truth behind that lust for blood perpetrated upon the streets of Whitechapel, Aldgate and Spitalfields.

For my part I received a standard education. I attended a comprehensive school for boys in Bethnal Green, before I worked as a trainee lining cutter in Brick Lane. That would have been around the same time that the curry houses were respectfully established and most of the buildings at that particular time were in fact manufactures for the rag trade, or "Sweat shops" as they became more commonly known throughout the 70's and 80's, after the Bengali migrants began to arrive in Britain.

But there was then, and still are many Victorian tenement blocks, dwellings and establishments, such as; The Old Brewery, The White Hart, The Ten Bells, The Hoop and Grapes, and a warren of cobblestone pathways, brick buildings and streets in which Jack the Ripper would have had to navigate during those dark foggy mornings of thunder and hell fire. For me personally, it is easy to imagine myself back in the days of Queen Victoria's Whitechapel and envisage the time when people would go about their daily lives, and where the gentile and upper echelons of society would frequent the drinking houses whilst out on a jolly. And the area well integrated with people from all over the globe. And among the decrepit buildings abject poverty and deprivation prevalent among the poorest whose objection would be to find that when they opened their eyes, they'd been confined to a forsaken hell hole with death and disease never far away.

I have always felt a profound kinship working within the confines of Whitechapel. My father's clothing factory was in actual fact situated at the corner with Greatorex and Whitechapel Road. When I was just fifteen-years old I would occasionally lean out of the old sash cord window in reverie during tea breaks and watch people walking up and down and across the busy main road where I would gaze at The Bell Foundry, set back at the corner with Fieldgate. My only knowledge of Jack The Ripper back then was what I had read when picking up local history books from the old school library at Daneford, which bordered the site of the Old Jago - known as The Boundary; and the place where I had spent many afternoons playing truant whilst smoking cigarettes on the bandstand with like-minded classmates. Back then I'd felt a distinct curiosity when I imagined ol' Jack the Ripper and his gruesome murders. As like most people the curiosity came about solely because he was never caught.

And a few years later, like a piece of metal drawn by a magnet, I was back working in Wentworth Street Market selling clothes. And as I stood by that market stall the curiosity found its way deep within me yet again. And now as I earn my living driving a London Taxi, I continue to find myself driving the Ripper trail with dedicated tourists. And I often visit Brick Lane for a curry, deliberately going off the beaten track on my way through. To me it compares to walking through the old town of Jerusalem, (which I have also done), following the steps that Jesus Christ once walked with the burden of the heavy cross upon his back. I adapted my mind to become engaged within the era I imagine myself to be in. And in this case as I walk the Ripper trail and spot the prostitutes clinging to those dark street corners, or hiding in the alleyways, spiritually I am back in 1888, and those astral bodies of Victorians palpable as the psychic elements linger above my head and encourage me to write this narrative.

John Lenard Stone.

Prologue

The Deadly Fruit of Original Sin

Switzerland 1923

Whilst a winter sun shone down over Vevey; a small town on Lake Geneva, there lay a retired surgeon tucked securely inside Egyption cotton sheets upon a wrought iron bed. Tall French doors to his left side covered by crimson drapes blacken the room. Wall-to-wall bookcases filled the room, whilst upon his bedside cabinet a brown medicine bottle and a fruit bowl containing grapes and blackberries a plenty. A clock with a noisy ticker showed the time to be 9.15. On the bedside cabinet to his right there stood a red vase made of glass, filled with fresh lilies and roses. A portrait of himself as house surgeon at the ducal palaces hung upon the wall above his head: The painting showed a distinguished figure of a man with gaunt facial features and a dark complexion, a good head of hair waxed into a centre parting. His big brown eyes, glazed and mischievous, whilst a hungry mouth beneath a bushy moustache turned up at either end. Also on the wall there were ornate brass candle holders fixed either side as their wicks flickered a small flame. A solid oak cabinet was situated along the wall perpendicular, and above, an oil painting showed a latino woman; she was wearing a red dress as she tapped her stiletto heels to dance the flamenco. The seventy-year old surgeon's head of hair now white as snow, as of his white handlebar moustache and bushy eyebrows that covered his sunken eyes, set within dark holes. His voice barely audible, a contrast to when he was a much younger man. His face permanently fixed towards the French doors.

The apparition of a faceless man stood reticent in a dark corner of the room, a cane held in his left hand. His garb; a shiny top hat and tails with ribbed wings that housed sparkling knives of steel and a waistcoat of ever changing colours, and not a single sound made. The surgeon, nor anyone else that entered the room could neither see, smell, or detect his presence.

The door squeaked noisily as it opened and an acerbic little nurse with cold watery eyes entered the room hurriedly. Inconsiderately, she slammed the door shut behind her, causing the doctor's heart to miss a beat as he shuddered due to the sound. Her garb; a dark grey and white pinafore and headress.

She immediately made her way towards the drapes and drew them back, before she opened the doors to let in a strong ray of light that shone straight through the room to light up the surgeon's pale face. His forehead speckled with beads of sweat, whilst his facial contortion showed his utter discomfort. 'Good morning, Doctor.' She greeted him in her usual bitter tone of voice as she turned to give him a brutal stare. He ignored her utterance and continued to fix his eyes upon the clear blue sky that he welcomed along with the freshness of the cold air that cooled his temperature. 'So how are we feeling today, then?' The mood inside the room was subdued and she showed little empathy towards him. 'Was it another uncomfortable night for you?' She stood and looked at him with her hands placed firmly upon her hips as she breathed a heavy sigh of reluctance, before she moved towards the bedstead and tucked in his bedclothes. 'Isn't the morphine helping you at all?' she asked as she stood shaking her head at him.

He groaned, for he was in pain as he tried to clear his airways.

'Suit yourself,' she mumbled as she readjusted the pillows behind his head, whilst she forced his head forward in the process of attempting to lift him up so he could have a clearer view of the outside world.

Insurbonite little wretch, he thought to himself as he twitched and winced. *How dare she speak to me in that tone. How can she expect a reply when I am clearly dying before her very eyes? Show some respect. I was chief surgeon to the royal household. A pioneer in my branch of surgery. I've served my country well and saved our King from certain death, ironically, be it from the disease that's about to take my own life.*

He shifted his eyes towards her as she quickly moved to his left side.

'There was an eclipse last night. It was such a wonderful sight to behold. To witness something like that over the lake. It was truly breathtaking,' she remarked poetically as she stood by his bed and steadily wiped his head with a damp cloth. 'Personally, I look forward to the springtime. I can't wait for the flowers to start blooming again… not forgetting the warm sunshine. That's what I miss most about England. The seasons are special.' She pushed her scrawny face into his then lifted his eyelids. 'We all have to face death one day, do we not? Nobody leaves this world alive, so it's no good fighting it, is it?. But then it probably won't affect you, will it? You'll be lying in cold obstruction, I'd say.' And as she exited the room the apparition moved into the light to reveal himself as the Elephant Man.

1

Aqua Fortis

1887

Isaac Angel opened his big brown eyes and checked the time on his pocket watch, situated next to him on the bedside table. The time showed it was 7am, so he climbed out of bed and slid into a pair of trousers and a shirt as he dressed himself for work. His wife Miriam continued to sleep as he stepped over to the small sink basin and ran the tap. He splashed his bearded face with water as he stood beneath the sash cord window that looked out across the backyards of surrounding properties. Once he'd slipped on his boots, he kissed his wife softly upon the head then quietly closed the door behind him as he left for work. Isaac was a boot riveter and worked locally within the area of Whitechapel and Aldgate.

Above the room where Miriam slept peacefully, Polish Jew and walking stick maker, Israel Lipski lurked as he paced the floor in trepidation inside his bedsit. He had waited for Isaac to leave the lodgings as he planned to force himself upon his heavily pregnant wife, once Isaac had disappeared from sight. And as she continued to sleep, she was soon awoken by a tap tap at the door. She looked up and asked herself who could be there?, so climbed out of bed wearing her nighty. Before she opened the door she asked, "who is it?" Israel Lipski stood grinning, mischief evident in his eager dark eyes, but answered her meekly.

'It is Israel from the room above,' he replied.

'What do you want?' she asked.

'I have summink to give you,' he said convincingly

She knew something was amiss as he held what looked to her like a small brown bottle containing liquid as she partly opened the door.

'I brought you summink to drink,' he whispered, as not to disturb other tenants residing inside the building.

'But I don't want anything to drink,' she replied irately as she stood holding the bump in her belly. She was angry because he had disturbed her from her sleep.

'Oh, but you must drink this, my love. It's for the baby, you see? It will be good for the baby,' he shot back at her as he forced his way inside the room and quickly closed the door behind him, whilst stealthily turning the key in the lock, as Miriam stumbled and fell backwards onto the bed in her retreat. And as she lay on the bed paralysed with him on top of her, she tried to scream as he covered her mouth with the palm of his hand, whilst with the other he took out a handkerchief from his top pocket and shoved it into her mouth to muffle her sound. She tried desperately to fight him off as he opened the lid on the bottle and poured what was aqua fortis down her throat, via the handkerchief inside her mouth. And as her eyes bulged with fear and pain, he forced her legs apart and inserted himself inside her, until he ejaculated. He then choked her to death with his bare hands as her body became limp and her face suffused. And as he continued to lie on top of her to catch his breath, her blood began to seep out from her mouth and her vagina to soil his filthy night shirt and long johns - evidence of his guilt. Israel Lipski had stolen Miriam's virtue and killed her unborn baby in one single moment of depravity and repellent selfishness, after months of watching her from his bedsit window above. And after he'd used up all his adrenalin he climbed off her and checked that he'd locked the door, before he laid himself down beside her on the bed and cried.

'I'm so sorry, my child. I don't know what came over me. I didn't mean to hurt you and your baby.'

The heavy banging at the door caused him to panic with the police screaming, 'Open up! Open up! Let us in... or we will force our way in! Come on, open up! I said open up, I say!'

In his discombobulation Israel Lipski hid himself beneath the wrought iron sprung bed, then curled himself up in the foetal position, as officers forced the door open and entered the room. The first officer entered and looked under the bed, only to find Israel

Lipski sobbing as he dragged him out by the scruff and told him he was under arrest for the murder of the young pregnant woman.

2

Isaac was standing at a bench. He was boot riveting when a woman living at the property entered the workplace frantic and screaming. 'Isaac you must come! It is your wife! She has been murdered!'

'What did you say?' he replied in shock at her words.

'It's your wife. Oh dear. She has been killed by another lodger. They've arrested him. Israel Lipski it was!'

'What did he do to her?' he asked as he picked up his jacket and rushed towards the door.

'They don't know. They just know she's dead, that's all,' she replied as she followed him out of the building.

***

At sixteen Batty Street people congregated outside the building as police officers held them back from entering to look at the dead person inside. And when Isaac arrived with the tenant he told them exactly who he was.

'I'm the husband of the woman who's been murdered,' he said. 'You must let me see my wife. I want to see her now,' he screamed.

'I'm afraid nobody will enter the building, until we've removed her body,' the officer replied stiffly.

'But I must see my wife! I am her husband! Please, you must let me see her,' he cried as he tried desperately to force his way through the entrance door.

'I'm sorry, you can't. I've been given strict orders not to let anyone pass.'

'When can I see her? I live here!'

'You can enter your lodgings when we have removed her body,' the officer reiterated.

Isaac was distraught with worry and remorse for the murder of his wife as he stepped back with his cap in hand and sat himself down on the cobblestone. He put his head in his hands and continuously sobbed until his brothers arrived and took him to their lodgings.

3

By August and with Lipski hanged at Newgate Prison, a drunken and livid Isaac returned to sixteen Batty Street with his two brothers and promptly entered the dwelling in a rage.

'Lipski,' he yelled. 'Where are you?' He climbed the stairs, until he was confronted by landlady Leah Lipski.

'What are you doing here? You cannot come here anymore. You are drunk. Now calm down Isaac and we'll talk about what he did to your wife,' she said sternly.

'It's all your fault. It's all because of you damn Lipski's,' he yelled as he lunged forward and dragged her by her hair down to the landing floor screaming blue murder.

'You must pay for my wife! I must kill you as my wife has been killed!' He began to kick her viciously about the abdomen with his size twelve metal capped boots, causing her to cough up blood, before his brothers decided to drag him away and out of the building, only to be confronted by two constables who'd had her cries. They quickly arrested him and dragged him to the cells at Leman Street screaming that she had to pay for his wife as she bore the same name as Lipski; the murdering Polish Jew who'd forced his wife to drink nitric acid as he raped her.

***

Inside an empty cell at Leman Street Police Station, Isaac sat upon the bed with his head in his hands. In total despair he sobbed into his lap, before he was approached by a burly bearded station sergeant.

'You, Sir, have committed a violent act upon the landlady at your abode at sixteen Batty Street. You will be escorted to the court in the morning, and you better be able to explain your actions, otherwise, you'll be going to the clink for the remaining year's end.'

'Isaac looked up at the officer, his eyes pink and his beard soiled with saliva.'

'She must pay for my wife,' he mumbled.

'You're Hungarian, I take it?' said the officer as he stood jangling his keys.

Isaac just nodded his head in agreement.

'So how are you gonna speak up for yerself in court, may I ask?'

Isaac just shrugged his shoulders, because his English was very poor, and he was frightened of what might happen to him upon his conviction for assaulting the landlady at Batty.

'Your vengeance towards that woman was not worth the effort, in my opinion,' the officer told him, before he walked off and left Isaac to introspect.

***

The next morning he stood in front of the Judge. His clothes ragged and his appearance bedraggled. He was but a shadow of himself in months gone by.

'Have you got anything to say?' the Judge asked him with a stern tone in his voice.

Isaac looked down at his feet pitifully and shook his head.

'Are you sorry for what you have done to this poor unfortunate woman?'

Isaac nodded his head in response as he tried desperately to speak, but without any utterances.

The Judge sighed in his agitation with Isaac, but told him he was to be bound over to keep the peace for one year. Isaac had agreed to comply with a "thank you" and a nod of the head, before he went to stay with his brothers, until he could afford another place of his own to live. But with his mind mangled and his anger festering daily he took to the bottle and began to sleep rough and live like a vagabond beneath the arches of Shadwell Basin.

February 1888

As Isaac walked the streets, lonely, angry and with nowhere else to go, he encountered middle-aged Annie Milwood as she passed him a filthy look on her way home from work. This caused a certain acrimony inside of him, so he took his vengeance upon her with his penknife as she hurried towards Whites Row, Spitalfields.

'Ay... you, whore?' he shouted after her, as she quickened her step.

'Oh go away, tramp. Leave us alone, wontcha?,' she cried as she turned her head to look at him.

'No, you leave me alone, whore' he roared back at her as he violently grabbed her throat, then stabbed her repeatedly in the abdomen in a frenzied attack upon her. 'You must pay for my wife,' he whispered into her ear, before she fell down on the stoney ground bleeding to death. Isaac's ears pricked up when he heard the whistle of somebody approaching. And within the minute the whistling constable spotted her dying on the ground covered in blood. He picked her up and rushed her to the receiving room at the London Charity Hospital nearby, where one particular doctor was on duty that night.

'I've gotta annuver one for ya, doctor,' the constable grumbled as he carried her in his arms. 'This is the second one this week.'

'Lay her over there on the bed and I'll stitch her up,' the doctor replied, all workmanlike in his fine west country accent. He cleaned and stitched her up and then sent her home, but she died two weeks later from her injuries. Isaac's rampage had begun as he attacked any woman that he suspected of being a whore.

4

August 1888

Above a vacant greengrocers shop situated along the Whitechapel Road, a large bird of prey flew off from its eyrie and hovered uninhibitedly above the rooftops. Upon the bird's head a top hat glistened under a coruscating night sky and a full moon. The bird's garb; a buttoned up waistcoat of ever changing colours of the rainbow as the red seal of the *Royal College of Surgeons* hung delicately from a thick gold chain beneath a cloak of purple ribbed wings that housed an assortment of knives of sparkling steel. And as the bird looked down upon the heavily congested streets and thoroughfares, he spotted the face of a lunatic; a heavily bearded, scruffy looking man who seemed to block the path of the women that encountered him as they attempted to pass by. The man was Isaac Angel, and he viciously uttered the words, gertcha! Before he jabbed his small penknife into their lower abdomen, causing them to scream out in agony and terror.

Noticing this, an officer of the law quickly put his whistle to his lips then immediately gave chase as he dashed across the busy thoroughfare then disappeared through Goodman's Fields towards Batty Street; south of the Commercial Road. The officer was soon ridden over by a speeding horse and cart as he tried in vain to catch the lunatic.

The bird looked down upon the heavily injured officer as he was brought to his feet by a group of stray children. Their large heads and small elephant trunks raised like trumpets within an orchestra brass section. But it was the bird's own childhood that he could see as he looked down and pecked wildly at his own chest with his long beak. And as he glided in mid-air, he gazed down upon the cackling whores as they lifted their petitcoats for the benefit of securing a punter whilst they asked for fawpence for sex. The bird began to drop oversized blackberries from the sky and into the most crowded areas where people congregated in small groups at the junction with Aldgate and Spitalfields. They scrambled and fought amongst themselves for the deadly fruit that hit the cobblestone at lightning speed, which caused huge explosions upon impact. The juice from the blackberries covered them in a thick red goo. And as the bird of prey continued to fly in circuitous fashion, he spotted two drunken vociferous soldiers in red uniforms. They were leaving The White Hart drinking house. The first soldier was broad shouldered and was tall; he bore thick orange whiskers, and a thick handlebar moustache that was turned up at either end. Clinging to his arm was a lubricious type, with long brown curls, sexy eyeballs and a large face. The other soldier was much smaller than the first and carried a full beard and moustache. He was smiling into the eyes of the other whore. She wore a black bonnet and was tall, fair, and her bright red lipstick illuminated her pallid face and round laughing blue eyes as she began to sing to him the words of an Irish folk song.

The bird of prey lost them briefly as they disappeared into the darkness of Gunthorpe Alley, situated immediately perpendicular to the pub. Some moments later they reappeared as the bird flew purposely above the rooftops. He recognised the carroty haired soldier with the lubricious woman. For he was not just any soldier, he was of the Queen's own regiment and highly regarded. The whore stood with her back to the wall at the entrance to a decrepit tenement block. Her dress pulled over her waistline and her bloomers around her ankles as she indulged the bearded soldier in an act of penetrative sex. The soldier's handlebar moustache splattered with his own saliva as the sweat ran down his sideburns whilst he sought a pleasurable conclusion for his generous sixpence.

The bird of prey landed stealthily upon the rooftop of the tenement block and looked down upon the couple as they physically interacted. He crouched down and began to masturbate as the soldier seeked his own eureka moment. But the soldier's ears pricked up as he stopped humping the whore. He put his nose in the air and sniffed the sudden waft of apricot as he listened to the bird's bronchial purring. Angrily, he withdrew himself from her vagina, then hurriedly pulled up his trouser zip, a look of mortification on his face as he turned to see what it was that filled his nostrils with this sweet aroma and caused him to lose his libido.

'Apricot,' he uttered aside as the whore let her dress fall down over her knees.

She asked him what the matter was? But he just ignored her sound, instead withdrew his sword from its scabbard and marched around in the darkness as he searched for the intruder that lurked within his midst. However, the soldier had paid her for her services and hadn't reached his precious conclusion. And in his disturbed mind he hadn't fully got what he'd paid for, so turned back to her in a fit of rage with his steel blade and plunged it deep into her abdomen. The sword went through her like a knife through butter as she gasped upon the sharp intake of the cold steel as her eyes bulged out of her head with deep terror.

'I dislike the smell of apricot,' the soldier growled at her before he made haste and disappeared into the smoke filled air.

And as she stood like a statue made from stone with her back towards the wall, she cupped her stomach in the palms of both hands, before she looked down at the blood that seeped through her fingers. She began to tremble and sob as she cried for help, but her sound was just a whimper in the darkness, until Isaac Angel claimed the space vacated by the murdering soldier.

'And this is for my wife,' his angry voice appeared to say as he entered the arena of hell and attacked the whore about the abdomen and face, and anywhere he could touch flesh, until she slid down the wall behind her and fell upon the stoney ground in a heap.

The bird of prey spluttered his torment as Isaac fled to a rumble of thunder and lightning that lit up the skyline and shook the ground beneath him. The bird nested upon her cadaver, and as he did so inserted himself inside her, before flying back to the eyrie above the old greengrocers shop.

5

Inside a reading room at the Royal College of Surgeons, set within Lincoln's Inn Fields, the tall, dark and distinguished surgeon was in deep conversation with Her Majesty's incumbent house physician. Over a glass of port they conversed concerning the gruesome murder of Martha

Tabram; the whore who'd been found by an officer of the law. She had been cut to shreds in Gunthorpe Alley to which a soldier from the Queen's regiment had since been accused. The constable found her a bloodied mess at the foot of the stairwell, after shrilling screams were reported coming from within the confines of the building. The accused soldier had been in the company of the whore according to a star witness; a colleague of the victim. She claimed that the soldier manhandled Martha and forcefully dragged her by the arm towards Gunthorpe Alley, which is directly behind The White Hart drinking house, the pub where they had been seen together that night, along with the witness and one other soldier. They had been seen drinking at the bar, according to the pub landlord when he was later questioned by detectives, one day after her murder.

1st Baronet, Sir. William Gull had deep, intense brown eyes and bushy eyebrows that covered his wrinkled eyelids. His hair cut back off his forehead, whilst a thick bulbous nose, and a thin top lip completed his large round face. He stood wearing a black suit and waistcoat that housed a gold chain, the red seal of the Royal College of Surgeons hung from it. He appeared vexed as he complained that the authorities urgently needed to find this star witness, since she'd agreed with the police that she was drinking at the White Hart with Martha Tabram and the two soldiers on the night in question, before Martha went off to have sex with the accused. The witness known simply as Pearly Poll, had personally picked out the tall, ginger bearded soldier, during an identity parade at Tower Hill Barracks, just two days later. Sir. William Gull revealed that police were sent to her abode in Cannon Hill, close to the Ratcliff's Highway, but she had since disappeared. She had allegedly received word that her life was in imminent danger, because the soldier she had pointed out at the parade was connected to the Royal Household Cavalry Regiment. This accusation had the Queen spinning with rage, and so a telegram was sent to the Home Office to find this whore and silence her immediately, before she spouted her story to the press, and in turn they published her lies. It could not be tolerated if the royal household were to become implicated in the prostitute's gruesome murder.

And as they walked shotgun into the opulent central hall, decorated with portraits of past pionering physicians a magnificent crystal chandelier hung delicately above their heads. Sir. William Gull told the doctor that his assistance would be required regarding this matter of prime importance to Her Majesty. He explained that one favour deserves another, and if he could locate this whore before the press got hold of her, he would be held in high regard upon his imminent retirement. With a nudge and a wink he maintained that he would personally endorse his qualities when he himself retires from his duties at the ducal palaces.

The doctor raised a brow, because he knew what Gull was saying in relation to "one favour deserves another," because the royal household had encouraged support for his patient's long term stay at Bedstead Square. Princess Alexandra had personally sanctioned his stay there. So he warmed to the idea of finding this particular whore named Pearly Poll. He was confident that it wouldn't take him long to locate her whereabouts, since he was familiar with the local prostitutes as they frequented the receiving room for treatment for various sexual diseases.

Sir. William Gull's eyes narrowed with evil intent as he warned the surgeon that if he should come into contact with this woman, or hear of her, he should, under no circumstances involve the authorities. He should instead telegram him immediately at his address in Mayfair. The surgeon's thick handlebar moustache twitched as he tapped his empty glass with his diamond ring finger, because he felt enthralled by this new role chosen for him. And he also thought that he should draw up a discrete plan to find her, because he knew he had all the right tools to carry out this secret mission to the fullest.

'Do we know anything about her appearance?' he asked.'

'Yes, we do, as a matter of fact. She is of Irish, or possibly Welsh descent. She's a brash, buxom redhead. Apparently she likes to sing when drunk, so it's been said.'

'It shan't take too long, I pray.'

'I hope not. However, remember this is an extremely sensitive matter, so please keep it under your hat. Not a word to anyone, otherwise, we may end up losing her for good, and that would be a grave concern to yours truly,' he explained as he looked up at the ceiling.

6

It was the night of the Shadwell dock fires. A lurid sky brought about by its omnipresence filled the east of London proper with a fiery miasma that forced the bird of prey to fly high above the smoke filled clouds as a rapid downpour fell down upon the luckless Polly Nichols, whilst she stood dripping wet upon a concrete slab by the entrance of The Frying Pan drinking house, situated at Thrawl. Her location, just fifty-yards east of Gunthorpe Alley, and where Martha Tabram had been savagely murdered with both dagger and sword only weeks ago. But her mutilation did not deter little Polly from her quest to find her doss, so she could pay for a bed come the early hours.

Polly Nichols was indicative of being a victim of a merciless Victorian circumstance; without job, nor place to call home - though there had been a period in her life when she did have security. Once married she'd given birth on five occasions, but had since split up with her husband,William, after one too many violent confrontations concerning her constant drunken behaviour and promiscuity. He'd stopped supporting her financially, so she was forced to work at a local infirmary, until securing a job as a servant for a middle-aged pious couple in south-east London. She was later released from her employment without references for allegedly stealing from them.

Polly held her position, wearing just a tweed jacket, skirt, and spring clipped boots as the rain dripped off the rim of her hat like a leaking tap. Her garb protected her little from the stormy skies above as she pressed her hand down on her bonnet with her free hand to stop it blowing away. And as she stood with her back against the door she became a constant annoyance to the punters who came and went.

'Get out the bleedin' way, will ya?' one angry coalman barked as he barged the door open with his shoulder and stumbled into the dimly lit den.

'Oh, sod off y'self,' she yelled back. 'Dontcha like me new bonnet, then? I'm wearing it just for you, you know, pig.'

'Yeah… and a thousand others more like.' a woman's voice shrieked back from inside the drinking house, followed by a sustained roar of laughter and clink of tankards. Despairingly, she turned away and staggered east towards Osborne and Brick Lane.

7

In the gardens of the London Hospital, under the umbrella of darkness, the solitary, unmasked figure of Jack stared down in reverie at the sodden flowerbeds buried in the earth. And as he stood in the continuous downpour, deprived of any form of normality, he remembered parts of his doctor's prognosis concerning his disfigurement. He recalled the day the doctor showed him off to the medical students at Bloomsbury Hall by making him stand naked in front of them. He also recounted some of the doctor's words from that day:

"{*The most striking feature about him is his misshapen head. On the top of the skull are a few lank hairs. The osseous growth on the forehead almost occludes one eye. From the upper jaw there projects another mass of bone; It protrudes from the mouth like a pink stump. The nose is merely a lump of flesh}*."

And as he hobbled along the waterlogged path with his cane held in his functional left hand indignation lurked deep within his psyche. His mind filled with terrible memories as he reflected upon the harsh treatment suffered at the hands of his owner Mr. Norman, particularly when he was exhibited as a fairground attraction in Belgium. He thought long and hard about the brutality he'd suffered inside the old greengrocers shop as he endeavored to find a place to hide from his own personal hell and the inevitable misogyny to which he had employed to protect himself against the spiteful women who mocked and treated him as a monster, a constant reminder of his wretched evil stepmother. He just wanted to hide in a place where he could never be seen by the people who mocked and mistreated him for his disfigurement. He sometimes wished he could have lived amongst the tribes that roamed the tropical forests of the world. But his actual jungle was simply a labyrinth of concrete and cobblestone they named Whitechapel.

Most importantly life had much improved since meeting the good doctor upon his escape from Belgium. For two years he'd managed to keep that little business card given to him by the doctor, after their initial meeting fours years ago. The card with the doctor's name stamped upon it in gold letters. He had taken advantage of his good fortune and bizarre oxymoronic existence. He knew he was now a protected species, surrounded by a ring of steel that reached all the way up to royalty. He was no longer the property, nor at the mercy of that drunken savage Mr

Norman; the circus owner, who stole his pittance and treated him inhumanely with regular beatings and spitefulness. And he was no longer residing on a cold damp floor at the rear of the greengrocers shop at 121 Whitechapel Road. He had been awarded since he was now an exhibit, belonging to his benevolent doctor and his highly strung students, and high society friends. He was the receiver of a greater welfare and a greater audience. A benefit that he'd always believed he was overdue, if he were to be gazed upon by a more respectful and appreciative audience who'd treated him with some dignity, due to his gift to medical science.

Since Jack's adolescence his life had been spent sleeping rough beneath the arches situated around Whitechapel. But now was his time and pay back an inevitability, because of the women who'd treated him so inhumanely. In his deprived mind it was time to pay the piper, and he couldn't wait a moment longer as his anger was allowed to fester in self-isolation. Those women had stopped him fom ever experiencing the one pleasure he so yearned for but would now experience in profusion - sex with women was his ultimate wish. The fawpenny whores who'd shunned him were repulsed by him and that simply added to his resentment of them in return. And this played heavily upon his mind as he searched for the missing ingredient to his comfier life at Bedstead Square. To feel the tenderness of a female was all he'd wanted, since love was the missing ingredient that had always spurned him, no matter what. And to raise a family of his own and live securely where he could walk freely and breathe a cleaner air without ridicule or prejudice, nor dread from the spiteful women who'd reminded him of his evil stepmother: She was the one human being who wouldn't accommodate him, since she could not bear to look at the sight of him any longer. And since his doctor had given him bestial books to read his mindset had gone into overdrive and he found it extremely difficult to distinguish fact from fiction, and fantasy from reality. His badly fractured emotions had become a paradox under a thunderstorm, since he'd felt a profound kinship with the daemon created by Victor Frankenstein in the novel, *The Modern Prometheus*. And while the daemon had also been in search of love, he too was aware of this void in his own living hell, and the oppressive anger to which the daemon's personal anguish was a constant reminder of his own depravity and treatment at the hands of those who'd taken control of his life.

8

While Polly Nichols rallied in raucous dispute with the heavily bearded deputy owner of the doss house, situated in Dorset Street, the doctor was busy attending to patients inside the receiving room at the London Hospital. The Shadwell dock fires had gotten out of control and every gypsy, tramp and thief from Whitechapel to Smugglers Highway, through to Shadwell Basin and beyond had arrived solely to reap the benefit of its destruction, as they pilfered and thought amongst themselves for the salvage left in its wake.

'Get out! And don't think about coming back, unless you've got your doss!' the deputy owner warned her, as he frogmarched her out of the door and back onto the dimly lit street.

'Oh, please save us a bed then, wontcha? Oh g'ron. I won't cause any trouble tonight, I promise' she pleaded as she sat in a small puddle of water on the cobblestone ground. But the deputy owner just turned his back and marched back into the kitchen without further ado. Polly Nichols fumed as she stared back at the open door with her bonnet in hand. Her pleas had fallen upon deaf ears, as he ignored her cries for a bed. And as he slammed the door shut, she was alone once more, and she knew, she simply had to get her doss to find herself a bed come early hours, be it with a stranger if necessary. 'Oh, never mind. I'll soon get me doss. See what a jolly bonnet I've got now?' she uttered as she climbed to her feet and stumbled off into the darkness of the night.

And as she made her way towards Osborne she bumped into a lady she knew called Emily. She was returning from the Shadwell Dock fires.

'Oh, 'ullo, Emily. Where've *you* been?' she asked whilst appearing light on her feet as she leant against the wall.

'Ullo, Polly. I've just been down to watch the fires down at the docks. I'm off home now. Where are you off to then?'

Polly was the assumed name she'd given herself upon her first arrest, when soliciting herself whilst being drunk and disorderly.

‘I’m out to get me doss, yet again.’ Polly slurred, upon opening her mouth to speak.

Emily noticed she was unsteady on her feet and showed her a look of disappointment as she tutted and shook her head at her. Emily was a well turned out woman and friendly by nature. She had known Polly for many years and knew how vulnerable the prostitutes were, especially with the volatile activity that was going on down at the docks. Tossers were infighting for anything they could lay their hands upon.

‘Well, you be careful, duck,’ she warned her. ‘There’s a rowdy mob lurking about out there tonight, that’s all I’m saying, duck. And I should know, I’ve witnessed those fires. You ain’t seen nothing like it, I‘m telling ya, girl.’ Emily showed her disbelief at what she had witnessed down at the docks. ‘People are wantonly attacking one another for stuff.’

‘Ay, you’ll never guess what, Emily? Polly replied. ‘I’ve had me doss three times already. Spent it all on gin, I ‘av’. Silly girl, ain’ I?’

‘You just make sure you get yourself that bed, that’s all, duck. You don’t wanna be stuck out here all morning. It’s bloody awful. Smell that stench.’ Emily said as she whiffed the air.

‘Nah, I’ll be alright, Emily. I’ve got me a new bonnet see?’ she declared, as she tilted her hat.

Polly was confident that she would secure her space inside a bed, even if it meant sharing with a man.

‘Aw, look at the time... it's two-thirty already,’ Emily commented as she gazed up at the church clock. ‘I must dash, duck. I’ll see you tomorra, yeah? And take care of yourself, especially if you're gonna be stuck out here all night long.'

'Yeah, all right then, Emily. See ya, doll,' Polly replied as she bounced off the wall tried to steady herself. Emily made haste, then disappeared into the fog. Polly continued on towards Whitechapel as the driving rain continued to fall down upon her.

9

Jack's nightmares continued as he looked down upon himself wandering helplessly beyond the hospital gardens and onto the busy thoroughfare, where he spotted Polly in the glow of a single street lamp. In askance, he noticed she wore a fancy bonnet as she raised her skirt to every male that walked past her.

'Business, Sir? Like what you see, do ya, Sir?' she exclaimed in clear desperation to attain her doss.

. 'Oh, come on darlin'… what's a matter, cantcha get it up for a pretty girl, then? I'm clean, you know!' But her cries for business only brought insults and sneers back in her direction.

But Jack was smitten by her, and fascinated by her beauty. And that rush of blood that ran through his veins towards his poisoned mind was completely overwhelming to him. He felt deeply frustrated as he stiffened. And as he hid in the shadow to watch her, he remembered the conversation he'd once had with his doctor, when he'd visited him after his morning rounds in the receiving room, and last Sunday was no exception for the meaningful conversation they'd had concerning the wretched whores who'd tormented him, particularly at weekends. He had complained to the doctor that he was having repetitive nightmares, and that he couldn't sleep because he was being hounded by these wretched women who loitered outside his bedroom window and teased him by lifting their dresses and showing him their breasts and cunny's. The doctor had told him that he would fix the problem. But he had felt exasperated and let down by his doctor's insouciance to do something, anything at all. The doctor joked that he should remove their breasts with his knife if it bothered him too much. He told him that he would personally show him how it was to be done if he really wished to learn. This proposition had caused Jack much anxiety and left him with a feeling of total rejection. The doctor had even given him a copy of his own medical book and urged him to read it, so he could learn just how to begin an operation using his steady hand. The doctor knew Jack had a good steady hand, because of his artistry with his model of St. Philip's Church. The model he was making from cardboard and being put together by Jack himself. He had convinced Jack that he had already achieved the main ingredient of any hospital surgeon - that of a steady hand. But then he complained to his doctor, that the surgical book had no romantic stories that he could engage himself with, unlike *The Modern Prometheus.* His doctor shared fits about that with his colleagues at the hospital and urged that if he really wanted to do an operation, he would have to do this without a love story involved.

But Jack was a fantasist and adored nothing more than to read bestial romance novels. It was one particular morning that his doctor had visited him, after a meeting with the Queen's own physician, Sir. William Gull, that he explained he'd heard through a medical colleague that Princess Alexandra was very upset, because the whores of Whitechapel were causing a nuisance and this was becoming embarrassing for the royal household in the eyes of the world. She had asked if something could be done about them? The doctor mentioned this to Jack, to which he had become distraught, since the Princess was the reason he had been given a room at Bedstead Square. It was upon her sanctioning of his stay there, so he felt duty bound towards her. The doctor had asked Jack what they should do about them, and how he might return the favour made by the Princess towards him? Jack was adamant that they should do whatever necessary to help Her Majesty in her plight to rid the area of these drunken whores. The doctor agreed with him wholeheartedly.

And as Jack continuously eyed Polly Nichols masquerading under the flicker of the gaslight, he pulled his cloak of sparkling steel knives over his head in discomfiture. He studied her as she stumbled along, then screamed as she fell down in a drunken stupor. She clutched a wine glass and swigged a mouthful of liquid, before she tripped and tumbled over.

Jack observed her every move and was completely overcome by her, since her pretty black bonnet made her look attractive from a distance, even so in the driving rain. And as he continued to watch her, he wondered what it might be like to have sex with her. He had only ever masturbated, and this fact made him feel extremely inadequate as his heart raced ten-to-the-dozen, and the butterflies danced around inside his stomach, whilst she oblivious to his eyes penetrating her as he watched her like a hawk watching its prey.

She cackled as she climbed to her feet, then positioned herself under the dim gaslight as she hummed a tune badly. Jack sensed that like him, she was desperately lonely. He felt with his physical wretchedness that he may be able to take her back to his room and have sex with her. He wondered how she might react if he were to try and speak with her? He would be gentle and kind and offer a gift of some sort. He would act as if he were a gentleman with a severe facial injury, due to an accident. And he could explain his hood and speech impediment if pushed to do so. And maybe they could become well acquainted? He could offer her a shilling if pushed to do so. He also thought long and hard about the unloved daemon in Shelley's novel. He remembered in the novel, the daemon was beaten and chastised for confronting his fears. He must not let this happen to himself. He would protect himself in case of that eventuality.

His heart pounded as a sickly condition filled his stomach with shooting pains. And with this in his mind, he wondered if something egregious was about to be played out upon the cobblestone streets opposite to the London Hospital. He began to hear the west country accent of the doctor ringing inside his head.

'Why does she make you feel this way, Jack? You have longed for this moment. Now go and get her. Go, before it's too late. She's waiting for you, Jack.' The voice of the doctor continued to drive him to despair.

'But it is very late,' he spluttered as he replied to the voices inside his head. 'And you said I am not to leave the hospital grounds under any circumstances.'

'Go and speak with her, Jack. And take your knife.' The doctor's voice was adamant that he should take his knife. Jack loved his knife, the one he used to shape his model of St. Philip's Church.

'But what if she screams? I will be exposed... and you will be vexed with me for that. Oh. Oh. Oh.' Jack stuttered at the thought of the whore and what he should do about her.

And as he maneuvered his way back to his small rooms at Bedstead Square he quickly collected his hood with a peaked cap attached, and picked up his knife from under his pillow where he caught a glimpse of his own distorted reflection. This forced him to turn his head away in horror, before he grabbed a handful of blackberries from out of the fruit bowl. They were given to him by his doctor upon his return from Dorset. Jack enjoyed blackberries and sometimes would use the juice for theatrical makeup, particularly when dressing up as a monster to frighten the young student nurses at the hospital. This was an idea given to him by the psychologist at the hospital, Dr. Tuckett.

10

Polly trudged back along the Whitechapel Road and was soon spotted by Joe Barnett, a tall, broad shouldered and fearsome looking man with a violent disorder. His penetrating small, icy blue eyes, deeply set inside huge black holes. His heavily chapped lips were purple in colour, like the satin that lined a viscount's cape. His prickly moustache soiled with stale food crumbs and mucus. He sported a deerstalker and a filthy brown sheepskin coat frayed at the trim.

Joe had strong affections for a whore he knew only as Mary Jane Kelly, however, he could not afford her since he'd lost his job at the fishmarket. So with this instilled in his mind, he would do anything to please her and win her affections for him again. For Mary Kelly; once his girlfriend, was now working as a prostitute from home where she lodged in a single room at Millers Court, Dorset Street, which laid within the boundaries of Spitalfields Market.

And when he spotted Polly he immediately began his approach, gesticulating, pointing and fist waving in her direction. Joe was a man unreceptive and besieged by venomous hatred as he bobbed and weaved back and forth, his eyes blinking uncontrollably. Highly vexed, he confronted her as she stood unsteadily on her feet inside the porch of the greengrocers shop at 121 Whitechapel Road.

'Oi, Nichols! I've been looking for you. I say, I've been looking for you. You still owe Mary for the garb - not to mention the bleedin' bonnet, I see you're still wearing.'

Joe Barnett possessed a speech impediment known as echolalia, and when enraged, he would soil his moustache with a frothy saliva, before running his fat furry tongue over his filthy black bush, akin to a lizard in a hot climate somewhere. He would follow this action by soiling the pavement, then wiping his mouth along his crusty jacket sleeve.

'Ah! Get off, will ya, Joey? Leave us alone for gawd's sake,' she shot back at him as she cowered inside the doorway.

Joe's huge frame towered over her like an almighty dark shadow in a terrible horror show.

'Tell'r she'll get her bleedin' money when I've earn't it proper. I can't even get me doss see... that's with this bleedin' bonnet on me head. You might as well take it for all the bleedin' good it's doin' us. I can't even give it away, let alone sell m'self for a few bleedin' penny 'ayp'nies.'

Joe spat blood as he watched her pathetic attempts to get to her feet.

'Well if you didn't spend it all on gin, you'd have it by now. And your doss, I say… You bleedin' well 'erd what I just said.'

'Well, I'll see'r m'self tomorra see.' she cried, as she attempted in desperation to keep her balance upon noticing his withdrawal. But her intake of alcohol meant she had little chance of realising where to put her hands when finding leverage to climb. 'And anyway, it ain't nuffing to do wiv' you, so keep your bleedin' nose t'y'self. Gor'n… piss off and leave us alone for gawd's sake.' Polly could certainly tongue lash when she was riled. Joe began to stir something inside her which made him retreat.

'Well, she ain't 'appy with you… I can tell you that for nuffing. I say… I can tell you that for nuffing, Nichols. She wants 'er money for that jacket an'all, and when I tell 'r, I've seen you tonight, she'll be 'opping mad I didn't collect, you get me? I say... you get me, Nichols?'

'Yeah, yeah, yeah, yeah,' she mumbled under her breath. 'You go and tell'r what I just said, gor'n.'

'You just watch y'self, Nichols, that's all,' he warned her, as he wagged his finger in a wasted fury, before he marched off in the direction of Commercial Street.

11

In light of his nightmare, Jack navigated the two steps outside his room, then hid himself in the darkest shadow as his eyes searched for the Nichols woman. He finally spotted her, and this time she was standing inside the doorway of the old greengrocers shop where he was once exhibited under the title - *The Deadly Fruit of Original Sin.* He noted that she was in conversation with a scruffy bearded man. The man he'd recognised from before was Isaac Angel; And once again he was highly vexed as he yelled abuse at her and threatened her as he poked his knife into her abdomen. He warned her of what he might do to her if she didn't leave him be. And with his eyes fixed upon them, Jack scurried along the perimeter wall as Isaac Angel suddenly vanished from view.

Yet again, Polly was disappointed at her bad luck. The realization of sleeping rough inevitable as she continued to occupy the porch to keep herself from the torrential downpour. But Jack still owned a key to the padlock at the rear of the shop, because he had decided to keep it upon his travels to Europe with his owner.

Polly suddenly heard the click of the lock from behind her; something strange as she turned her head towards the door now ajar. And in fear of Isaac's return she fell back towards the door now open and entered the darkness that awaited her. The rancid smell of rotten vegetables was a humdinger to her, and the cold chill made her shiver. But this was no ordinary situation as she began to hear a sound that she could not recognize - for it was alien to her and filled her with deep dread as she shuddered and squirmed on the spot to which she occupied. But her little legs could not move her away from the bronchial purring that frightened her half to death. And as she sniffed the putrid air to fathom what it was she could smell through her senses, the waft of apricot confused her. Jack used apricot perfume in abundance to quell the ghastly odour that followed him everywhere.

Another click of the lock and immediately upon her spin she lunged towards the door and tried desperately to open it, while up from the ground behind her and in the shadow of unthinkable darkness the diminutive figure of Jack stood in all his unmasked glory, holding a lit Bunsen burner in his good hand, his knife in tother. And as he reached out to her he placed his diseased hand upon her shoulder. She gasped and buckled at the thought of someone standing behind her. Nevertheless, she wanted nothing more than to see who it was that stood purring over her shoulder like a wild cat. But something inside her warned her to stay calm and so she obeyed her primal instinct as Jack began to plead with a splutter.

'Please do not turn around. I don't want you to be frightened.'

'Who is this?' she asked, her voice brave inside a tremble.

'I'm Jack. But I do not want to frighten you. I am badly disfigured.'

'Well I don't frighten easily, I don't mind tellin' you that for nuffink'.'

'Good because I am not going to hurt you.'

'O, why not? What'd ya want, then?' She knew something was not right with this unexpected meeting. For the first time in her life she became speechless.

Jack brought his knife under his cloak, then put his diseased hand over her shoulder to place it in front of her. His hand filled with blackberries as he put them under her nostrils. She looked down at his oversized hand and quickly realized that she had to get away as quickly as possible. She was horrified and had never seen a hand so huge in her whole life.

'I brought you these. I thought you might like to have them,' Jack spluttered, hoping they may settle her fears. But Polly Nichols was in no doubt her life was in imminent danger as she frantically stuffed them into her mouth to stop herself from screaming.

'Ta,' she uttered, her voice shaking with fear. She masticated and scoffed the blackberries all in one go as a thick red juice began to escape and trickle down her chin in vertical fashion, which created a thin red line that ran down towards her scrawny neck and into her cleavage.

Once again Jack could feel the sickness inside his stomach as he deliberated whether or not he should disappear to whence he came. But it was too late, there could be no turning back, not now. His mind telling him that he had to see this through, and that she had to die for him so he could indulge her without her screaming blue murder.

'Can I go now, kind, Sir?' she pleaded as she dared not turn round in fear of what she might be confronted with, since she knew this was no ordinary meeting, and definitely not the place to be with this unrefined gentleman who stank of apricots and struggled to be gracious and charming.

'I hoped you would not mind, but I have been watching you from the hospital where I live.' Jack attempted to enunciate his words as he continued to stand behind her, breathing down her neck like a vampire in a horror book. 'I thought you looked quite beautiful under the gaslight. And your bonnet suits you so, if you excuse my impertinence.' Jack endeavored with his speech as best he could. But this meeting wasn't working out the way he had expected. It was too challenging and the barriers betwixt too great a task, even for a literate and learned person like himself.

'Nah, why should I?' she replied, with an air of grace this time. Polly suddenly realized that the man standing behind her was in fact the Elephant Man. She knew there was a deformed man living at the hospital. It was the word on the street, and everyone knew about the existence of the Elephant Man. This truth made her feel a little more steady on her feet as she regained her confidence.

'I used to live here, inside this shop. It isn't very nice, is it?'

'It's cold... and it stinks, or you do.' she replied hastily.

He peered over her shoulder towards the door; once his window to the outside world. She could hear the rattle of his lungs as he did so.

'The doctor's there are very kind to me. But I get very lonely.' He paused for an intake of breath. 'Sometimes I return here to sleep, particularly when I feel so alone. Are you lonely?' he asked her.

But Polly had lost her will to accommodate this unexpected meeting with the Elephant Man any longer. Her patience had grown too thin, and her fear had transposed into intolerance, because she was desperate to claim her doss, and a bed for the night was her priority, and she knew she had little time left to acquire it.

'You're not that elephant freak everybody's talkin' 'bout, are ya?' she shrieked as she cracked under the mounting pressure. 'Is it business you're after, then?' And as she twisted her neck to look at him, to her horror Jack stood in all his unholy glory. His eyes pink and aflamed, magnetised under the reflection of the steel blade in hand, and his penis fully erect. She stood aghast as his tongue shot out of his mouth, like a lizard about to feast on a mealworm in a jungle somewhere. His knife raised above her head brought down upon her like an axe that split her lip in the process. She screamed in agony as her decaying teeth extracted from her mouth and flew through the air before she collapsed to the floor in a crumpled heap.

'*She's all yours, Jack. Take her before she wakes.*' The voice of the doctor inside his head continued to berate him. Jack's broken heart raced as he knelt down and parted her thighs and his cloak slipped from his tiny shoulders. He inserted himself inside her in search of warmth from her virgina. To feel that intimacy with the opposite sex was all he craved for in search of the missing ingredient to his better existence.

And as little Polly Nichols laid unconscious from the strike upon her, he sank his oversized thumb deep into her throat and pushed down with all the strength he could muster. She gasped as she took her last breath. And as he looked down upon her lifeless body and realised she was gone he released himself and brought his knife to hand, ready to search for the answer behind his disfigurement as he sliced her throat from ear to ear, and then in total hopelessness he tore into her abdomen in continuous downward strokes with his knife pointed southwards whilst calling out for his mother with a chilling scream that could only be imagined in a Sherlock Holmes novel. And as all his strength was lost in a frenzied attack upon her, his anger finally quelled as he crouched over her ripped up cadaver and wailed until he could no more. A savage murder inside the dwelling where he had once been held in captivity by that freak-show host Mr. Norman would not sit well with his doctor. And as Polly bathed in her own blood from her deep wounds, Jack scurried back towards Bedstead Square like a rat in an open sewer. For Polly Ann Nichols lain on her back upon the cold, damp floor of the old greengrocers shop. Her eyes wide open and the mutilation of her abdominal area the final chapter in her quest to find her doss.

12

And as the bird of prey hovered over the smoke filled docks, once again he spotted that same deprived man Isaac Angel. This time he was sitting upon the banks of the river, a bottle of methylated spirits in hand and a look of utter despair upon his hardened bruised face. Isaac had found himself living inside an abyss of unremorseful violence, misandry and loathsomeness. His life had taken a stranglehold upon him to which he could never free himself from the entanglement of his viciousness, because when he had returned to the address at Batty Street he'd kicked Israel Lipski's sister half to death in retaliation for the murder upon his wife and unborn child. It was from that day, after he was bound over to keep the peace for one year thereon that he swore to avenge his wife's death and live as a lunatic throughout his years in Whitechapel. However, time was up, and one year had passed since his court appearance. And by now he'd attacked dozens of women with his penknife. He'd lost count of the injuries he'd inflicted upon them and the ones that had died at the mercy of his unstable mind. He had become psychotic upon a mission to attack whores so they may never carry a child. The womb a personal place of sanctuary for the unborn, except for his unborn child, had been forced to drink nitric acid during an unwarranted attack upon his pregnant wife. Isaac's motive was to deter whores from offering their rotten flesh for pleasure, since this absent pleasure had been stolen from himself and his wife, deceased. In his mangled psyche the whores were a source of disgusting food for the filth that utilised their sexual fruits. And most of all they were unfit to give birth, or promote their filth on the streets of London.

And as the fires continued to rage the bird of prey looked down upon the luckless Isaac as he stumbled and fell down upon the banks of the Thames in a drunken stupor. He was broken and had lost the will to continue living in an atmosphere of utter neglect. During the past year he'd become a repellent murdering scavenger living off the breadcrumbs and the stale potatoes that he'd stumbled across inside the old greengrocers shop, or stealing from unsuspecting drunken whores who he'd viciously attacked with his knife.

And as he lay face down in the mud, he smashed his fist upon the sludge in self-pity as he stretched his arms to pick up the biggest of stones that he could see. Encouraged to take his own life he climbed to his feet and stumbled towards the suffused river that was lit up like a mirror aflame. He stared up at the lurid sky as the rain saturated him in turn, and for all his sins that had been recopence for his wife's murder he knew it was a time to repent and die. His legs began to buckle beneath him as he stared down aimlessly at his distorted reflection in the glistening red river where all he could see was the face of his beautiful dead wife Miriam; her hair white as snow and her eyes coruscating a brilliant hue of aquamarine.

'Come my love. Come with me. I've been waiting for you.' Come to me,' he heard the sweet sound of her soft voice as she beckoned him towards her. His face lit up like a sparkler as he bore a huge grin and followed her instruction as he entered the freezing cold water, now covered by black petals that rode the crest of the soft flushes. Isaac had finished his talionis and with his pockets filled with the heaviest of stones.

The search for the missing link to his happiness had begun as he forced himself towards his retreating wife and further away from the bankside and into the drench and depths of his death.

***

Upon reaching the hospital gardens, Jack looked down at the flowerbeds as his nightmare scenario continued to disturb his sleep. He sweated profusely as he twitched and jerked inside his own skin, and a sudden rush of blood to his brain caused his nightmare to cease and he awoke. His mind tortured by the lack of ability to comprehend fact from fiction. And that acute anxiety that had built up inside him over many harsh years of brutality, long before the slaying of the unfortunate whore.

He climbed off the bed and lifted his pillow to see if his knife was still put there; and so it was, so he grabbed it, then slid on his hood situated on a hook behind the door. And as he babbled incoherently, he opened the door wide and hobbled out and back towards the flowerbeds in the hospital gardens.

'Oh dear. What have I done?'

But the gruesome murder of Polly Anne Nichols had been far more surreal than his current nightmare, since Jack had found himself in a state of psychosis, a detatchement from the truth as to whether he had done anything wrong, or if he'd even left the grounds of the hospital at all. But on this occasion it wasn't the entrance of a tenement block at Gunthorpe that he'd witnessed a bloody murder. It was but the greengrocers shop, and an unfortunate prostitute whose only crime was to dance and sing beneath the gas lamp as she clutched a wine glass and appeared pretty under the gaslight. And through his nightmare commenced the same fiendish brutality as he pondered whether or not he'd committed a deadly crime.

***

During the early hours of the same morning, unaware of his patient's truancy, the doctor was attending to the injured inside the receiving room at the hospital. Upon taking a break, he decided to visit Jack in his rooms at Bedstead Square. He knew Jack wasn't sleeping well, because he had been complaining to him about his wretched nightmares. The time was 3.30 a.m when the doctor opened the door at Bedstead Square and looked inside, But Jack's bed was empty - he wasn't there at all, and neither was his knife.

However, the doctor knew exactly where he might find him, since he had gotten to know that Jack liked to visit the old greengrocers shop from time to time, and it was just a short walk across the road from the hospital's main entrance. He went to see if Jack was there hiding in the dark like he enjoyed to do immensely. Although he had taken Jack away from the greengrocers shop, he hadn't quite managed to take the greengrocers shop away from Jack. And like a magnet drawn by a piece of metal, Jack was drawn to his deprived past. Upon entering the greengrocers shop he stood inside the darkness and called out to his patient. 'Jack! Jack! Are you here, Jack? I've come to take you back to your rooms.' And as he searched deeper with a lit match held aloft he stumbled upon a bundle beneath his feet. It was the ripped up body of Polly Nichols.

'Good heavens!' He knelt before her and struck another match, before he covered his orifice with a handkerchief when he spotted her horrific injuries and a pool of blood that covered his shoes. He climbed to his feet then immediately exited the shop without once looking back. The doctor hurried back to the hospital and quickly entered the backyard, where a horse-drawn carriage was situated without driver. The doctor climbed aboard and raced back to collect her mutilated body. And after putting her cadaver inside the carriage, he drove her to Bucks Row, just a stone's throw from the main entrance to the hospital. He laid her body out as if she had been there previously. He then returned to the receiving room to carry out the rest of his duties while Jack laid deep in slumber and imagined himself as that bird of prey elevated above the rooftops over Whitechapel and beyond.

13

As Jack continued to sleep, the plumped up pillows positioned behind him stopped him falling into an asphyxiating position. Due to his neurofibromatosis and Proteus Syndrome. He had little choice but to sleep this way. If an accident should occur and his head were to roll off his pillows, he would most certainly die from the lack of oxygen to his brain. And his doctor was aware of this fact and made sure the nurses on night duty had taken responsibility for his sleeping position. He ordered them to check on him throughout the night and during early hours. However, as it was a raucous weekend because of the dock fires, the nurses were run off their feet, whilst the night porter was off duty. With this in mind, Jack had sought his opportunity to leave the hospital undetected, as he often did at weekends and on bank holidays.

And when a nurse entered his room, her tormented eyes and gaunt facial features reflected her resignation to the fact that it was she that had been given the unforgivable task of making sure Jack had his first bath of the day. Even with the apricot perfume, Jack still carried that foul, musty odour. She gazed at him briefly whilst she shook her head in irritation as he continued to snore, loudly enough to wake the dead. His bronchial purring, a reminder of what she had to put up with in her own daily life as his personal day nurse.

'Jack, wake up! It's eight o' clock!' She spoke in a high pitched and bitter tone of voice. 'We've all overslept this morning! It's time for your bath!' she went on, as she sniffed his odour with a look of utter disdain evident upon her pale complexion.

'Come on now, Jack!' she said as she marched over to his iron sprung bed and put her orifice deep in his earlobe. 'Now, come on! This is not a flippin' doss house, you know!'

But Jack had experienced her intolerance several times. He knew if he ignored her for long enough she would eventually give up the ghost and continue with her other main duties.

And as he began to stir, he moved his enlarged hand away from his ear, then turned his head towards her. He recounted his nightmare and that exhilaration he'd felt as a result of being a bird of prey. And he thought about the gruesome murder that he'd committed earlier that same morning with his knife that he used to shape his model of St.Philip's Church.

His eyes shifted as he watched her filling his bathtub with water from a large metal jug.

He pretended to be asleep as she leant over his desk and opened the rotting sash-cord window. The creaking sound from this exercise disturbed him and made him flinch, whilst the smoldering reek of the Shadwell Dock fires lingered in the air, as a ray of dust particles lit up the tiny room when they swirled and danced in clockwise inside a transparent tube that stopped at the door opposite to the window.

The nurse made her way back into the adjoining room, situated immediately to the left of the door. She returned clutching a bath towel, then suddenly stopped in her wake, because she was awed by the tall, lean figure of the doctor standing inaudibly in the open doorway. His mischievous dark eyes narrowed as he scanned the room with a purposeful intent, highly suspicious of Jack and the murder that he believed his patient had comitted in the early hours of that same morning. He wanted to catch Jack, before he had time to concoct a story in connection with his knowledge of the butchered prostitute. She had been found by a police constable doing his rounds during the early hours, discovered only yards from the hospital in Bucks Row.

The doctor had read the gruesome details in the morning journal, and was perturbed to know why his patient had visited the greengrocers shop during those hours that he wasn't in his bed.

The doctor was groomed, handsome, and a pioneering surgeon in his field of medicine. His thick moustache neatly trimmed, and his hair waxed into a defined centre parting. He stood in fine posture, dressed in a long black astrakhan coat. In his right hand, he clutched a felt hat - his Gladstone bag held in t'other. The red seal of the Royal College of Surgeons hung delicately from a thick gold chain inside his waistcoat pocket.

And as he checked his solid gold timepiece, clipped to his lapel. The morning journal figured under his arm. It was clear from the doctor's appearance that he was a man of high distinction, a man with mighty connections and far reaching tentacles.

He deliberately loosened his grip on his Gladstone bag so it fell to the floor with an almighty crash. His surgical instruments chung as they danced around upon impact. The sound of those steel instruments echoed inside the small room as the noise bounced off the walls, loud enough to make his patient's heart miss a beat. And as the doctor observed the nurse going about her morning duties, she readjusted her headdress when she looked up at him in melancholy, for she was highly embarrassed for her lateness this morning.

'Oh, excuse me, Doctor, but you half frightened me to death standing there like that,' she remarked with guilt evident on her suffused face. 'I wasn't expecting you to visit Jack so early this morning. He hasn't had his bath yet,' she continued to say, as she bowed her head in shame for her impertinence.

'That's all right, Nurse. I shan't be a moment. I just want to speak to Jack in private, if I may? If you would be so kind as to give us a few minutes alone?' he replied in his fine west country accent.

'Oh, of course. Certainly, Doctor. Just give me a shout on your way out,' she replied compliantly, before she closed the door shut upon her exit.

The doctor was the sole protector and confidant to his patient. It was with regret that he had been busy of late and didn't have the opportunity to visit him more regularly, since his heavy workload had taken up most of his free time.

He grinned inwardly, then chuckled briefly upon her exit, before he stepped forward and placed his hat and journal down on the wooden desk directly in front of him. He began to search for clues as to his patient's involvement in the death of the prostitute. And as he did so, he thought in retrospect that day that he first set eyes upon his patient. It was four years ago inside the old greengrocers shop. And when he first laid eyes upon him for the price of a shilling, he recalled how he stood awestruck at the forlorn silhouette and subject matter known as *The Elephant Man*. A frightful moment that stirred something unearthly inside his soul and encouraged him to have mercy upon this person's depressive demeanour. An atmosphere of neglect and abandonment filled his mind with regret, followed by a desire to offer his benevolence towards this grotesquity, which could only be envisaged in a ghastly nightmare. He wondered just how Mr. Norman could have been so cold and callous to treat a human being as a freak show monster, though himself intrigued to know more, particularly concerning the disease the subject had exhibited for him personally, as he stood like a dangerous animal, chained to a cage with only a Bunsen burner to keep his tiny bones warm. Mr. Norman had made Jack stand half naked in trousers ten times above his size, as he showed off this most unpleasant specimen to those who were willing to pay for a viewing. Thoughts of Mary Shelley's novel, *The Modern Prometheus,* sprang to mind for the doctor. Victor Frankenstein's creation had encouraged him to act out this private meeting, set up by a psychologist working at the hospital. He had known firsthand how the doctor had an absurd fascination with monsters, demons, and freaks alike, due to him telling that he once kept a monster he named Hermon when he was a child growing up in Dorset. This fact made him feel that he was fated to meet Jack from the outset, and that was why he'd given him his personal business card.

And as he looked upon the dimly lit and dampened wall, there stood the sign that engraved itself like an indigo burn upon the doctor's sensational mind, and the sign that the diminutive figure of The Elephant Man would have sited every single day of his imprisonment at the greengrocers shop, whilst appearing in captivity. The sign that read:

14

The doctor regained his thoughts, then checked Jack's cloak and hood that he'd hung on the back of the door. He searched for clues as Jack opened his eyes and stared over at him, expressionless to his favour. The doctor knew his patient had been out, because his cloak and hood was still damp. He could feel Jack's eyes upon his back and grinned, before he turned and passed him a knowing grin.

'So you're finally awake, then. A better sleep this time, was it?' he enquired with a hint of excitement in his voice tone. Jack's splutter could only be properly deciphered by the doctor, since he had come to know his patient well enough over the last two years or so. Sunday morning tea's and long chats usually concluded with them talking about one bestial novel or another that the doctor had got for him from the hospital library. Their conversation would depend on which book Jack was reading at any particular time. Other books he'd been reading included: The Man in the Iron Mask, and, Dr. Jekyll and Mr. Hyde.

'Oh, I had the most terrible nightmare again, Doctor. It was the most wretched nightmare I think I have ever had in my entire life.'

'So, what happened?' he replied as he stepped towards Jack's bed.

Jack climbed off the bed then searched helplessly for his slippers. The doctor found them and picked them up, then placed them by his patient's feet.

'Well, I dreamt I was a bird of prey again. It was completely surreal. I was actually pecking at my own flesh. Oh, it was such a vivid nightmare, Doctor.'

'So which bird of prey were you this time, Jack?' the doctor asked as he scratched his chin in wonder.

'Oh, I'm afraid I don't know. I could have been an eagle or a vulture,' he replied, seemingly disorientated 'I'm not certain which bird I actually was.'

'Could it have been a peregrine?' the doctor asked willingly.

'Oh, I don't know what a peregrine looks like, Doctor. Can you show me a picture of one?'

'Of course. A peregrine is a type of large and powerful falcon. It has long pointed wings and a short tail.'

'Oh, I really don't know,' Jack replied.

The doctor placed his hand upon Jack's shoulder and smiled at him for not knowing which bird of prey he might have been during his nightmare. It was important, because the doctor was also suffering nightmares, except his nightmares were due to his concern for his patient.

'Would you mind sitting down for me, Jack?' the doctor asked in a more austere tone this time. He felt some complicity in the death of the prostitute, because he had moved her body to protect his patient. It was also the headline in all morning journals. He was intrigued to know if Jack was involved in her death, or he had witnessed the person who had committed the crime. He knew Jack had good reason, since he's studied his patient better than anyone, with the exception of Mr. Norman of course - Jack's previous owner. Mr Norman once revealed to the doctor why he'd kept the Elephant Man in chains: "It's for his own safety, as well as the safety of others," he remembered Mr Norman telling him. And when the doctor had asked him why he thought he was a danger to others, Mr Norman replied, "well, wouldn't you, if your own mother abandoned you?"

'Yes, of course. What is it, Doctor?' He sat down on the wooden chair in front of his desk and looked up, like a house pet needing to be stroked.

'This morning at approximately three-thirty, a.m, can you enlighten me as to where you were and what you were doing?' The doctor could barely contain himself, because this was exactly the sort of game he enjoyed playing.

'At three-thirty?' Jack spluttered as he stared through the window at the half built church.

'Yes, precisely.'

'Well, I couldn't sleep at all,' Jack replied. 'Because of my nightmare.' Jack knew he had an advantage over his doctor, because of his expressionless facial features. And he knew it was virtually impossible to decipher whether he was lying, or telling the truth. He was able to conceal any lie if pushed to do so. And he knew he should act as he usually acted, not to reveal any sign of change in his character - good or bad. It was this astuteness that had saved him from certain death many times, long before he'd met his caring doctor and began his new, comfier existence.

'You poor, poor soul. So, what time did you finally get to sleep, then?' The doctor asked as he stood towering over his patient, his hand firmly placed upon his shoulder as he stared introspectively out of the window.

'Oh. Oh. I can't remember what time exactly. I think it was about that time shortly after I remember climbing onto my bed. I recall the church clock striking the hour at four if that helps?' Jack asked, before he began to bore the doctor about the time he went to bed. 'The sky was very red, and it was raining heavily. To say… I mean, it was quite frightening to see a bright red sky with the rain falling so hard at the same time.'

'Was it indeed?'

'Oh yes.'

'That's because those fires were deliberately started down at the docks. I'm sure the stench will linger for days to come.'

'Why do you ask what time I went to bed, Doctor?' Jack had to know if the doctor suspected him of something that he wasn't sure of.

The doctor looked down at him with great empathy, because his sixth sense told him that his patient was most definitely the doer of the whore, but he needed to be totally convinced before commencing a cover up. The game was to prise it out of him beforehand. And he was really enjoying the psychological battle behind their conversation even more so.

'So, a wretched woman; a prostitute was savagely murdered in the early hours at around three thirty this morning. And it just so happens that you were seen in the gardens by one of the night nurses after that time.

She says, she saw you hobbling in the grounds. Did you not see, or hear anything?; A scream, or a squeal… anything that may have caused you to feel alarmed for your own safety?'

'No, I'm afraid I did not hear, nor see anything, apart from the usual disturbances,' Jack replied.

'Thank heavens for that.' The doctor sighed in relief. 'I was quite worried about that, because my first point of plan this morning… after I spoke with Dr. Llewellyn, was to check to see if you were still sleeping,' the doctor revealed. 'Obviously, you must have retired rather late as you were in deep slumber. You were snoring to the sound of ten large men after four a.m.'

Jack continued to stare out of the window and wondered what might happen if the doctor knew he'd spoken to the whore. But he couldn't decipher if it was during his nightmare he'd actually killed a whore. He would need to inspect his knife. But that would have to wait until the doctor leaves, he thought to himself.

'Oh, it is such a fine morning, Doctor, don't you agree?' Jack's sudden burst of enthusiasm made the doctor smile to himself, though he remained silent as he studied his patient's persona throughout. 'I'm sorry, but I cannot remember anything regarding the early hours, after I went to bed. I'm sorry if this has caused you any embarrassment,' Jack continued to say, as he continued to look through the window.

'Dr. Llewellyn informed me this morning that the injuries inflicted upon this poor unfortunate woman were likely to have been committed by a left handed person, the doctor replied with renewed vigour. 'And you… well, your good hand is your left hand, is it not, Jack?'

Jack's reticence spoke volumes concerning the murder of the whore, as the doctor continued to bombard him with more relevant facts regarding her death.

'And according to Dr. Llewellyn, the knife used to cut her throat was not such a sharp knife either,' he went on.

Jack pretended not to hear the doctor as he gazed at his model of St Philip's Church, situated on the table in front of him. Jack used his knife to shape the card for his model and knew it was the reason for its bluntness. He had asked his doctor on many occasions to have the knife sharpened, or get him a new one, but the doctor had refused, on the basis that he didn't completely trust him.

'Incredibly, they have moved her body to the greengrocers shop, where you used to work for that wretched man. I'm going over there later to examine her injuries for myself.'

'The greengrocers shop? But how?' Jack asked in dismay, because in his nightmare he'd had sex with her inside the greengrocers shop and witnessed her being butchered by the bearded man that he keeps seeing in his nightmares. *How could that be, if she was already there?* He wondered if his doctor was teasing him.

'Well, they found her lying dead in Bucks Row, during the early hours. And as you know, that's just a stone's throw from my hospital.'

Jack now realized that his doctor suspected him, even though he had explained himself.

'All right then, Jack. Stand up for me, please,' the doctor demanded using a formal tone this time.

Jack wiggled out of his chair and stood still.

'Now, I want you to know that I'm going to be visiting you more frequently from now on. I realise, I've been very busy of late with my workload and with the students. I made a solemn promise to look after you and I shan't shut you out any longer,' he confessed.

Jack stood helplessly as he contemplated his dire situation. He knew a still mouth would be best served by acting in accordance with his low self-esteem.

'Would you mind if I continue with my model now?' Jack asked, as he looked up at his doctor.

'All right. But I will visit again this coming Sunday.'

'Thank you.'

'By the way, which book are you reading at the moment, Jack?' the doctor asked as he bent down to pick up his Gladstone bag.

'The Modern Prometheus,' Jack replied excitedly.

'Ah. Shelley. Good. And have you read any of the chapters in my surgical book, yet?'

'No.' Jack answered quickly. 'It is too complicated.'

'All right then. I shall take it with me when I leave.'

Jack picked up the small book from the stack on the table and handed it back to the doctor.

The doctor slipped the little brown book into his medical bag then closed it shut.

'You won't take the other one with you, will you, Doctor? I haven't finished reading it.' Jack implored the doctor not to take this particular book. It was his favourite book, because it was the one that he related his own circumstances to, like that of Victor Frankenstein's creation.

'No, I'm not going to take your books from you, Jack, so stop panicking, please,' the doctor replied shaking his head in annoyance at him. 'It's truly a magnificent setting, is it not? he remarked. 'You know, Switzerland is a very beautiful country… very beautiful indeed. Just as Fort William in Scotland. They are two of the most scenic places I can think of right now.'

'Oh, can you take me there, Doctor?' Jack began to clap his hands excitedly. 'I want to go to Switzerland. Will you introduce me to Dr. Frankenstein? Oh, how wonderful it would be to meet Dr. Frankenstein,' Jack cried out in elation.

The doctor laughed hysterically at the possibility of meeting a fictional character.

'No, I'm afraid we cannot meet Dr. Victor Frankenstein, Jack. But I will take you to Fort William if you wish, though not in the immediate future as I am far too busy with my work overload. I have patients queuing for me in the receiving room right now,' the doctor told him as he opened his medical bag and took out the morning journal. He placed it down at the foot of the bed.

'Oh... and by the way, I've been arranging your holiday for the month of November. I have some very dear friends in Northumberland who would love to meet you. They will treat you as one of their own. I'm sure the fresh air will be good for your bronchitis,' the doctor told him as he opened the door to leave. 'All right, nurse. I've finished with this scholar. He's all yours.' The doctor exited the room as Jack picked up the morning journal and read the front page headline:

HORRIBLE MURDER IN WHITECHAPEL!
WOMAN SHOCKINGLY MUTILATED!
HEAD NEARLY CUT OFF!

Jack swung his head back in horror, then gazed out of the window as he stood in reverie.

'Oh, oh, you poor, poor thing,' he spluttered.

The nurse entered the room with a large jug of water. She marched immediately to the bathroom and began to fill his bathtub.

'May I see the chaplain after my bath please, Nurse?' he asked pathetically.

'Yes, of course you may,' she replied abruptly.

'I feel so wonderful this morning. I would like to share my joy with the chaplain, if I may?'

'Now come on. Let's get you washed and dressed. You smell awful today. It's much stronger than usual. You must have been sweating profusely in your sleep.'

'Yes, I was,' he uttered, as he hobbled towards her.

15

Four-thirty in the early hours and the alarm clock rang out a deafening sound as it rattled upon the bedside table, next to the doctor's side of the bed. He awoke and immediately threw an arm out from under the blankets and smashed his hand down to turn off this horrible, disturbing noise. His wife lying next to him tutted her annoyance, before she shuffled and shifted in her position to face the sash cord window, then buried her head beneath the sheets.

The doctor yawned and climbed out of bed in his navy blue, silk pyjamas, then stood rubbing his eyes. He looked down at his wife sleeping peacefully, then tiptoed around the bed towards the window ajar, where he peered through the drapes and looked down upon the dimly lit Wimpole Street. He spotted the driver of a Hansom cab situated at the corner with Wigmore.

The driver sat like a cardboard cut out; motionless as he waited patiently for his first fare of the morning. This area of London was mostly inhabited by people who worked in their private medical practices, and that included the doctor's home address, since he would often treat private patients at home at Wimpole. Also this part of London was known for its brothels, where the wealthier of gentlemen could visit for a discreet session in massage and other relaxation pleasures.

The doctor's address was within easy reach of the London Hospital. The journey topographically, "as the crow flies," door to door from his address to the hospital main entrance. And he would sometimes walk this route in half an hour flat. However, today he'd decided to cycle to work, as he had plans to stop off along the way and chat to some of the street whores in relation to locating Pearly Poll's whereabouts. The only question upon his mind this morning was which hat he might choose to wear.

So whilst the birdsong twittered in the chill of the dark foggy morning, a whispering breeze filtered its way through the velvet drapes, cooling the warm temperature inside the room. The doctor grabbed his dressing gown off the hook at the back of the door, then quietly left the room, leaving his wife to continue in her slumber in peace.

The problem was that the doctor wasn't sleeping well at all, since his patient had burdened him with his persistent bird of prey nightmares. And what he'd stumbled across, upon his visit to the greengrocers shop in the early hours, truly affected his mind. The savage death of the Nichols woman was playing heavily upon his psyche. He believed Jack to be the perpetrator, and he'd realised that his patient was stalking the local whores at weekends when he could abscond from his abode. The murder of the whore had taken its toll upon the doctor, to such an extent that his own mental state had been compromised. He'd become momentarily forgetful and irritable, short fused and temperamental, and he had begun to lack empathy towards his patients at the receiving room. He knew he was losing his mind and had turned to drinking absinth, and dabbling with the drug laudanum during shift patterns. This extreme pressure he was suffering was because of his loyalty towards his patient, and his understanding of why his patient had perpetrated such a violent deed against that whore. The doctor could no longer sleep for long hours without waking up in hot sweats and bouts of disorientation and fatigue. He'd even prescribed medication for himself, to calm his nerves. All was not well with the doctor. All he could think about were those two gruesome murders in recent months. However, the one thing that he was sure about was his responsibility for Jack, because he'd taken it upon himself to be his protector, as well as his doctor. He'd made a promise to look after him, and not allow harm to be inflicted upon him by those who viewed him as a monster. And if Jack had indeed taken the whore by the knife, the doctor knew he would have no choice but to support him from those who might be baying for his blood, before they came marching towards the hospital with their torches aflame.

And his worst fear came to light one day in the receiving room itself, when he'd overheard a conversation between two female patients. He'd heard one say to the other that a deformed man living at the hospital had savagely murdered the whore found dead in Bucks Row. This accusation had made the doctor extremely worried and he wondered if somebody had spotted Jack at the greengrocers shop that night. He knew he had to act quickly. To distract attention away from Jack and the hospital in case his patient had been reported to the authorities. The whispers and rumblings were becoming evermore frequent among patients and staff at the hospital. And he knew he'd better fix this problem before the authorities began to take note of these earth shattering chatterings amongst local folk. "*Before you know it, they'll be coming for Jack with their ropes and gibbet at the ready,"* he'd told Dr Tuckett one day in confidence.

And if Jack was going to be arrested, it would most definitely destroy everything the doctor had worked for in his entire life. His own reputation was hugely at stake, and his position as chief surgeon would be at an end if Jack were to confess under duress and then charged with her murder. He simply could not allow his patient to be the focus of these recent chatterings any longer. He would have to take drastic measures to shift the attention away from the hospital and lay blame firmly at somebody else's door.

16

Upon leaving the house at five o'clock precisely, the doctor looked up at the blackest of skies. He dragged his bicycle with him and placed his Gladstone bag inside the tray affixed to the handlebars. Being an avid cyclist, he enjoyed the quickness of which he could move around London, particularly during the warmer climates, and cycling to work saved him the price of a Hansom cab. On most winter mornings he would usually take up the option of hiring a horse-drawn carriage upon getting to and from the City of London.

And as he reached the junction with Norton Folgate and Shoreditch, he dismounted and walked his bicycle across the deserted road. He walked down Commercial Street, since he was in no particular hurry this morning. And as he pushed his bicycle along the pavement through the morning mist, he stopped to check his timepiece at the corner of Hanbury. A primal instinct caused him to look towards the Christ Church where the muffled sound of a bearded gentleman dressed shabby gentile appeared to be extremely animated. The doctor noticed he was clutching a dagger in his right hand. The gentleman soon vanished into Spitalfields Market, so the doctor twisted his bicycle and walked down Hanbury Street. He noticed the three story tenement blocks were set upon either side of the street when he spotted a whore of around 5ft, conspicuous as she leant her head forward as she stood inside a footpath, leading to a backyard of house at number 29. The whore wore a straw bonnet, long skirt, and a woolen overcoat.

The doctor stood and watched her intently as she brushed herself down after she'd indulged with the gentleman he'd seen dash across the road just moments earlier. He contemplated if she might be the whore he'd been asked to find on behalf of Sir. William Gull.

After noticing his silhouette, the whore called over to him as she beckoned him towards her with a quick wave of the hand. The doctor acknowledged her with a mischievous grin and cruel intent upon his unsettled mind. So he leant his bicycle up against the wall situated next to the alleyway and lifted out his Gladstone bag from the tray before he began to engage her.

'Ullo there.' She spoke quietly, but her voice was shaky. 'What can I do for you this morning, Sir?'

'Oh, I'm not sure just yet,' he replied in a baritone voice. 'Maybe you can tell me your name?'

'I'm Annie Chapman,' she replied. 'Now how would you like a nice warm suck to start your day, then? It'll only cost ya fawpence. What'd ya say? I'm good, you know.'

Her forwardness was impertinent, he thought to himself as he stared knowingly into her blue eyes.

'Oh, come on, Sir. It'll only cost fawpence. It's your lucky day, cos I'm feeling really generous as you'll be my last this morning. And you look like a nice clean gentleman if you don't mind me sayin', I must say. And you don't get many of those 'round these parts at this time of the morning, I don't mind tellin' ya that either. You look like a doctor to me.'

The doctor snarled as he contemplated the odds of her being the one Sir. William Gull had wanted him to locate.

And as she opened her coat, she lifted her skirt and showed him her naked thighs.

'See for y'self, I've got the cleanest thighs you'll see anywhere 'round these parts, that's for sure,' she said proudly as he looked down at her naked flesh.

'I see.' He stepped forward and grabbed a handful of her vagina and squeezed hard.

'No!' She gasped with displeasure, for his forcefulness caused her much pain. But he felt calm inside, like never before. He was now positively sure he was ready to begin the job of finding Pearly Poll, whilst at the same time protecting his patient from the authorities, should someone give his name up to the police. 'Oh, please be gentle, Sir, for gawd's sake. I bruise very easily,' she asked mercifully, before he released his grip and wiped his hands upon a clean handkerchief.

'Very well,' he replied as his body towered over her small frame.'

He suddenly felt a cold chill run down his spine as the lank hair on the back of his neck stood up. He wiped the perspiration away as the exhilaration of this unexpected meeting had given way to any attempt to think rationally. He began to think about how he would save her blood for his own initiation ceremony as part of the reinvention of an old society that he was looking into. And he would show potential members wishing to enrol just what they would have to do to prove their allegiance.

'Follow me then. Come on. I promise you won't regret it. You can ask anyone round these parts and they'll all tell ya the same thing. I'm the best when it comes to using my mouth. I'll 'av' ya cummin' in seconds, that's a promise,' she expressed with confidence, as the doctor stood cradling his Gladstone bag.

'Will you?' he replied in wonder at her promise to fulfill him with pleasure. 'Will you indeed?'

'Oh yeah,' she answered with an eagerness as she knelt down and unbuckled his trouser belt.

'Wait! Just a moment, please.' he implored her as he moved her hands away from his genitals.

'What's wrong with you now?' she gasped as she stared up at him.

'I heard something... a noise perhaps? Didn't you hear that?'

'No. I heard nuffing. Anyway, it's normal to hear noises 'round these parts. D'you want this, or not?, cos I'm not here just for the hell of it, you know.'

'Yes, of course,' he replied as he looked over the fence and into a backyard to a house with a creaky shed door. 'Firstly, I must do something.' He unclipped his bag and took out a handful of blackberries, then handed them to her.

'What are they for?' she asked, as she stood up and took them from him.

'Blackberries. I thought you might like to try them. I hand picked them myself from Dorset,' he said.

'All right. I'm bloody starvin'. But don't you go thinkin' I'm doin' anything just for a few blackberries, you know' she retorted as she bundled them into her mouth. 'Hm. Ta,' she spluttered with her mouth full.

The doctor watched her with a deviant cold stare as the juice seeped from her mouth and rolled down her chin in a straight line. And as he waited for her to finish masticating on the juicy blackberries, he checked his timepiece. Now was the time to ask her if she knew of the prostitute he'd been chosen to find.

'Do you know of a woman who goes by the name Pearly Poll?'

'No, I don't. Who's she?' she replied as she scoffed the remaining blackberries.

'Pearly Poll,' he reiterated irately.

'Why d'ya wanna know that anyway? My mouth not good enough for ya?'

'It's not that. I just need to speak to her. It's important that I find her.'

'Well, I dunno,' she replied.

'Come on then. Let us start the day with a little self-gratification, shall we?' he said as he put a leading hand upon her shoulder. The old clock from the brewery struck the half-hour as he frogmarched her further into the pitch black alleyway. And as she bent down to take him, he stealthily reached into his bag and took out a piece of cloth he'd saturated in chloroform: And as she took out his penis, he grabbed her by the throat and forced her up against the fence, where he pressed his cloth filled with chloroform into her face, so that she couldn't breath. And with impetus he viciously pressed both his thumbs deep into her throat, causing her to lose consciousness. She was now putty in his hands as he squeezed harder and further into her throat.

A sinister thought crossed his mind as he lifted her off the ground and held her tightly, like a rag doll in a puppet show, until she had completely gone and was at the mercy of his evil intentions. And as he released his grip she fell to the floor in a crumpled heap. Suddenly, he heard the sound of a shed door closing and opening nearby. He stood quietly for a moment in the darkness, aware of this unwelcomed sound, before he knelt down beside the whore and lifted her clothing above her waist. In the darkness he cut her throat with a methodical precision, using the sharpest surgical knife from his bag. He bided his time as he began to cut into her abdomen and lift out her inners. The blood seeped from her wounds to form a small puddle beside her as he began a disembowelment, cutting clinically downwards into her stomach and removing her organs.

He was a master surgeon - an appendectomist. He knew how to work in the dark and had done so in the past. He could do his job blindfolded, since he'd studied the anatomy of the human body as well as any surgeon in the land. And after he removed her liver, he took out her womb with his bare hands and placed them in symbolic fashion around her cadaver; a message for the authorities that Jack could never be capable of performing such an operation of this type.

And when he was done with her dissection, he cleansed his knife on a piece of cloth taken from his Gladstone bag, before positioning her arm across her chest as a symbol of respect for her. And as he climbed back on his bicycle and rode astride like a bat out of hell towards the hospital, Jack's nightmare continued as he flapped his ribbed wings of steel over the rooftops, to keep up with his overprotective doctor who surely by now had saved him from accusation and hell fire.

17

The doctor stationed himself behind a solid oak desk inside his office. He was in the process of writing a letter, using red ink syphoned from a small glass jar upon the table. His desk, positioned opposite the entrance door. A sash cord window situated behind him looked down onto the busy Whitechapel Road, and a coal fire burned beneath a mantle to his left.

And as he continued to write, the sound of horse clatter and shouting outside interrupted his concentration, so he stared up at the crystal chandelier hanging above his head, before he took a sip from his small glass of port. He picked up the letter then climbed to his feet, before he began to recite the words he'd written down by adopting his most finest Dorset dialect.

"[Dear Boss,

I keep on hearing the police have caught me but they wont fix me just yet. I have laughed when they look so clever and talk about being on the right track. That joke about Leather Apron gave me real fits. I am down on whores and I shant quit ripping them till I do get buckled. Grand work the last job was. I gave the lady no time to squeal. How can they catch me now. I love my work and want to start again. You will soon hear of me with my funny little games. I saved some of the proper red stuff in a ginger beer bottle over the last job to write with but it went thick like glue and I cant use it. Red ink is fit enough I hope ha. ha. The next job I do I shall clip the ladys ears off and send to the police officers just for jolly wouldn't you. Keep this letter back till I do a bit more work, then give it out straight. My knife's so nice and sharp I want to get to work right away if I get a chance. Good Luck

Yours truly

Jack the Ripper

Dont mind me giving the trade name.

PS. Wasnt good enough to post this before I got all the red ink off my hands curse it.

No luck yet. They say I'm a doctor now. ha ha.]"

The doctor stared down at his letter introspectively, until a noise behind the door caused him to look up. He dropped the letter inside the open desk drawer then quickly closed it shut.

'Enter!' he called out from his position. A pretty, young nurse opened the door and stumbled in. She was dressed in a long grey flannel skirt and white pinafore.

'Well, what is it?' he asked using an abrupt tone of voice.

'There's a man - a gentleman to see you, Doctor,' she replied.

'All right then. Show him in. Don't keep the man waiting any longer than necessary, woman.'

'Yes. Sorry, Doctor,' she replied slightly embarrassed by her indecision.

And as she exited the room, he buttoned up his shirt, then walked around the table, where he positioned himself to receive his guest; a tall, middle-aged gentleman, who bore long side whiskers and a carrot coloured handlebar moustache and beard. He wore a deerstalker, and a tailored tweed suit, and clutched a black leather bag in his free hand, and a clay pipe hung delicately from his lips.

Upon recognising who the gentleman was immediately, they shared a grin and greeted one another in a brotherly fashion as the doctor stepped forward and gave him a welcome hug. The pale face nurse acknowledged their friendship with a smile and then quietly left the room, closing the door behind her.

'Thomas, old boy. Good to see you. Good to see you at last.' The doctor was chuffed to pieces as he hadn't seen his dear friend in over six months proper. He had missed his quick fire wit and quirky romantic tales of infidelity in Middle England, particularly since the doctor had relocated from Derbyshire to London. They'd attended the same school in Dorchester, headed by Dorset poet and philanthropist Sir. William Barnes. And they would often recite one or two of the old teacher's verses over a glass of port, or brandy when they were out on a jolly. The poem they always enjoyed reciting was *Blackmwore Maidens,* because it was a favourite among the locals in Dorchester.

Thomas removed his pipe from his mouth.

'Likewise, old boy... you old scholar you.' Thomas exclaimed in a broad west country accent, before he dropped his bag at the foot of the table as they began to recite the old teacher.

' "The Primrwose in the sheäde do blow,
The cowslip in the zun,
The thyme upon the down do grow,
The clote where streams do run;
An' where do pretty maidens grow
An' blow, but where the tow'r
Do rise among the bricken tuns,
In Blackmwore by the Stour." '

'Ha! Well, well, well. So, you finally made it to London. I must say, I've really missed you, Thomas' the doctor remarked as he took up his position behind his desk. 'Did you find the lodgings I got for you?'

'Oh yes, I did. Batty Street. The landlady gave me the keys. I stopped to drop off my luggage.'

'And how did she seem?' the doctor asked.

'Good enough about it.'

'Very good.'

'You know something, it hasn't stopped raining from the time I left Christchurch to the time we passed Christ Church here in the east of London,' Thomas quipped as he took his pipe from his mouth.

'Ha! Very good, Thomas. You made the connection, I see?'

'Oh yes. I certainly did, dear fellow. I'm ahead of you, you see.'

But the doctor already knew the connection concerning the street names and thoroughfares within the confines of Whitechapel and that of Dorset; Commercial Point in Dorset, he linked with Commercial Street in Whitechapel. And Christchurch he'd already linked to the Christ Church in Spitalfields. And then there was Dorset Street, t'boot.

Thomas had a great sense of humour and his purpose for visiting London on this occasion was to complete his denouement for his novel. Thomas was searching for added inspiration and thought he may find it in London's east end somewhere.

'Ha! Excellent! Let's drink to that, old boy.'

'Of course. How impertinent of me.' The doctor climbed out of his seat and stepped over towards the drinks cabinet.

'So what can I offer you to drink, then, Thomas? You must be exhausted,' the doctor asked as he picked up a bottle of port.

'I'll just have a glass of that poison you're holding, if you'd be so kind, old boy,' Thomas said in jest. 'I'm as dry as a carcass in the Sahara,' he went on to say.

'Of course.'

He filled two glasses, then handed one to Thomas, before they raised a toast.

'To London!' they cheered in sync.

The doctor slumped back in his seat and studied Thomas from across his desk, as he fiddled with his clay pipe.

. 'So where are all the pretty maidens I've been hearing about?' Thomas looked up and asked, before wetting his beak with a sip of port.

'Ha! All in good time, my dear friend. All in good time,' the doctor replied as his mischievous dark eyes peered over the rim of his crystal glass as his moustache twitched.

'Well, I'd rather hoped the journey from inside my carriage wouldn't be more exhilarating than my destination. All I've seen thus far is filthy whores falling about the streets in a drunken stupor, just waiting to get ridden over by some thoughtless driver or other. Not to mention the huge fat bellied pugilist I spotted punching hell out of some poor old fellow as we rode past Aldgate Pump. It reminded me of a sketch from one of Hogarth's paintings.' Thomas exclaimed, as he crossed his legs and relit his pipe.

'Welcome to the East-end of London, Thomas,' the doctor replied. 'You see, I've pretty much gotten used to it, though I do wish they'd make the effort to lock up these gin filled whores. You know, Whitechapel has great potential to become a thriving part of London's corporate future.

'Due to the price of the real estate, no doubt,' Thomas replied without prejudice.

'Quite right,' the doctor replied.

And as they began to reminisce about the old school where William Barnes had taught them both literature at one time or another, Thomas spoke about his forthcoming novel and how he'd hoped to finish it before the coming year. The doctor was attentive and interested, because he was in awe of Thomas's creative writing skills. He aspired to Thomas in more ways than one, but felt his book might meet with serious challenges, since it pushed the boundaries and wasn't much like anything he had written before. The doctor questioned if it may cause a stir amongst his most devoted followers.

'That's the whole point,' Thomas told him. If we regretted everything we ever did, we'd never do anything.' Thomas examined the doctor's thoughts concerning regret. 'If you could turn back the clock, what would he have done so differently?'

'There are too many to mention,' the doctor replied as he shook his head in belated wonder. 'And I wouldn't want to burden you with them all.' The doctor paused to introspect for a moment. 'Anyway, enough of me harping on... how would you like me to show off the beaten track, Thomas?' the doctor asked as he began to rock back and forth.

Thomas threw out his outstretched arm containing his empty glass.

'Of course, I'd love that,' Thomas replied.

The doctor climbed out of his chair and refilled their empty glasses. He handed one to Thomas before sitting back down at the table.

'Yes. Actually, I brought my map of London with me this time. I thought I might take a stroll along the Victoria embankment and survey my bearings,' Thomas replied with an added enthusiasm. 'And did you know there are two Dorset Streets in London? It says so, here on my map.'

'I do. In fact, both of them are significant, because they are just a stone's throw from me when I am at home, or at work.'

'Oh? How is that?' Thomas raised a brow, though he was well aware the doctor had two abodes, because most surgeons around the country had more than one address. He was interested to know exactly where they were in relation to one another.

'In fact, there is Dorset Street which lies off Commercial Street, behind Spitalfields Market... that would be opposite to the Christ Church.'

'Yes. Go on. Go on,' Thomas interrupted the doctor's flow.

'The other one is in Marylebone... a stone's throw from my house in Wimpole, though they are very different in every respect.' He went on to explain to Thomas of another location; a newly rented lodgings he'd taken in Batty Street, situated off the Commercial Road: A more sedate part of Whitechapel.

'That's truly fascinating. You see... this is just what I love about London. It's so expansive, but yet so dynamic. A Metropolis... bursting at the seams with its energy. So much history and dark tales of intrigue and misadventure, and that's what I aim to capture in my forthcoming novel.' Thomas felt elevated at being in London for the autumn. He believed it to be just the kind of inspiration needed for his book.

'Yes. And one more thing I forgot to mention, Dorset Street here in Whitechapel is referred to as Dosset Street,' the doctor stated.

'How truly remarkable,' Thomas replied with added enthusiasm.

'Yes. It's where most of the doss houses are situated, you see. And believe me, you can smell the filth all the way to the main entrance downstairs.'

'Oh, come on now, old boy. I came to London to see all its unholyness for myself, and all of London I shall see. Ha! And you *will* take me off the beaten track, or I shall never bring my hand picked blackberries for you again.'

'All right then, agreed,' replied the doctor. 'I shall personally take you to Dosset Street myself and hand you over to the baying fawpenny whores.'

Ha! Old London Town!' Thomas raised his glass. 'And to all the Dorset men who assist in her prosperity!'

Thomas slammed his glass down upon the desk and opened his bag. He took out a brown paper bag containing a bunch of blackberries. He handed them across the table to the doctor, and in turn, he dropped them inside his desk drawer on top of the letter he'd written to the press agency.

'So tell me, how are you getting on with that little creature of yours?' Thomas asked casually.

The doctor explained just how Jack had improved with his speech, and how he liked to chat about a certain book he might be reading, particularly the ones he enjoyed the most.

'Would you like to meet him?' the doctor asked.

'I'd love to.' Thomas replied, before he put his pipe back in his mouth. But he spotted a certain abstention in the doctor's eyes. That troubled glare that Thomas had never seen before. He knew his friend well and wondered if there was an ongoing situation which was troubling him. 'Oh, come on now. What's going on with you? I know you better than you think. You've got acrimony written all over you. Come on, out with it, old boy. What's going on with you?'

The doctor's eyes suddenly became mischievous and fixated. He deliberated whether it would be wise to disclose recent events to his friend. He pushed his chair back and stood up, then gestured towards Thomas to be quiet as he put a finger to his lips.

Thomas immediately realised something wasn't right when the doctor marched over towards the door.

'One moment,' he whispered, before he opened the door and called the nurse. She appeared in his eyeline, 'Make sure I'm not disturbed, is that clear?' he demanded as she nodded her head in agreement.

'Yes, Doctor, I will,' she promptly replied.

'Good.' He closed the door and returned to his seat.

Thomas pulled his chair closer towards the desk. He knew the doctor was about to disclose something of substantial proportions. He'd been reading in the journals about the ongoing murders in Whitechapel of late, and his sixth sense told him this may have something to do with that.

The doctor took his seat back at the table, then paused before he spoke. Thomas was all ears as the doctor leant across the table.

'Something dreadful has happened since I gave him Shelly's novel to read. I think I've actually managed to stir the beast within him.' he said eagerly.

'Yes, well. But what for heaven's sake? How?' Thomas felt the tension mounting quickly inside the room, so wanted the doctor to expand further with his shocking reveal.

'It was him. He did it. He bloody well went to the greengrocers shop where I first found him and did for her,' the doctor explained. The excitement in his eyes was overwhelming for Thomas to see as he shook his head in dismay at what the doctor was telling him.

'He did what, for heaven's sake?' Thomas replied in irritation.

'He ripped her up… the whore Polly Nichols,' the doctor replied, as he stared eagerly at Thomas.

'What... he told you this himself?' Thomas asked with a disbelieving frown.

'No, of course didn't. But I know he did it. And he knows damn well he did it,' the doctor answered in satisfaction with himself as he began to rock back and forth in his seat and nod his head in confirmation of his belief.

'What the hell has gotten into you, man? Surely you're not suggesting he's the Ripper, are you? The poor creature can hardly walk for heaven's sake.' Thomas began to chuckle at the idea of the Elephant Man being able to rip up a woman and leave her in such a state as that of the Nichols woman. 'No,no, no, I can't have that.'

'"*Ecce Homo,"* Thomas.' I know. I agree with you wholeheartedly, but I am saying exactly that. The trouble is, I've let myself down. I too have become deeply involved.'

'You what, man?! Because you gave him a book to read? Look, that doesn't make you an accessory to a murder. No, no, no!' Thomas replied in askance as he removed his pipe from his mouth.

'I know. But listen to me, Thomas. I had a deep conversation with him some time ago and he actually revealed his interest in medical science to me. So I gave him a copy of my surgical book to read. Now, put that with Shelley's novel and there you have it. He believes in his mind that he is Frankenstein's unloved daemon. He even asked me if I would take him to meet Victor Frankenstein.'

'But that's pure fantasy. You must have facts, old boy, before you accuse your patient of such a ghastly crime' Thomas replied with a vigorous shake of the head.

'To be honest with you, Thomas, I've hardly slept a wink since I last spoke to him.'

Thomas sighed a heavy heart. 'But to murder?' No, no, no. What are you saying, old chap? Have you gone and lost your mind?' I think you might be barking up the wrong tree there... unless you have concrete evidence that he did it.'

The doctor spread his arms across the table and took a deep breath.

'Thomas, these whores aren't your pretty maidens like back home. These women are fawpenny whores. They're the scourge of our great city,' the doctor shot back at him. 'Quite frankly, they've been a bloody menace to him. It's no one's business what he has to put up with… what with his own mother abandoning him at infancy, just because of his wretched disfigurement. And then there was the eschewment of his shameless stepmother, all because she was reluctant to be seen out with him. He gets hounded late into the early hours when they come to his window and taunt him. If you ask me it's enough to drive anyone to complete insanity. One could hardly blame him now, could they?' The doctor's eyes suddenly became black, his face pallid.

Thomas leaned forward ardently and spoke with fervour.

'Look here, I sympathise with you, I really do. But I will not sit here and condone what you are telling me, because if this is true, you simply cannot involve yourself in some kind of witch hunt, just to protect that repellent little creature.'

Despairingly, the doctor threw his head in his hands, then ran his fingers through his thick black hair. And as he stared through his parted digits, his face became contorted, desperate and tormented.

Thomas stared down at his drink and wondered if he'd been poisoned, before he slid back in his seat, afraid at the image of the doctor being possessed by evil before him.

'It's too late. I'm already deeply involved,' the doctor growled in a deep, devilish tone of voice that bounced off the walls and penetrated Thomas's ears.

'What?! Christ! What's happening to you, man?! What if you're apprehended? What will happen to you, then? You damn well need your head examined! For Christ's sake get a grip of yourself, man!' Thomas cried as he jumped out of his seat and attempted to escape from the room. He tripped over the chair leg and fell down. And as he looked up at the doctor standing over him there was a protracted silence that followed as the doctor turned and walked back to his desk. His eyes returned to their normal shade of brown as he stared down upon the busy street. Thomas climbed to his feet in anticipation of what the doctor might do next and stepped towards the door.

'Let me remind you of how terrified Jack is, because of his mother's abandonment of him at birth. I even had the psychologist examine him thoroughly. He informs me that Jack's misandry is due to his mother's desertion of him.'

'Even so,' Thomas replied exasperatedly, as he picked up his crystal glass from the table and quickly downed the rest of his port.

'The authorities know the whore was murdered by a left handed person that so happened to have used a blunt knife. They believe he fed her with grapes, before he murdered her. In fact it was blackberries he gave to her. One could never have expected him to perform such a savage surgical attack upon her. I even examined her myself and was completely taken aback by the extent of her injuries. He must have lost his mind completely when he attacked her with his knife.

'If what you are saying is true, then you should turn him in at once. You have no choice. I said he was a monster right from the very beginning. I just knew you would get your fingers burnt one day with this freak of nature person, the moment you set eyes upon him. He is the deadly fruit of original sin. No wonder his owner made him wear chains,' Thomas retorted in pure frustration with his friend the doctor.

'I shall not turn him in at all. I am responsible for him. And I made a promise to protect him. I will stand by that pledge if it damn well finishes my career in medicine. We were fated to meet, and we will be fated when we part company.' The doctor knew there was no way back. 'Anyway, I've decided to send him away for the last two weeks of November. The fresh air will do him good.'

The doctor stood up and snatched Thomas's glass from his hand, then poured two more glasses of port. 'There is something else I must tell you. Oh my dear God,' the doctor uttered as he bowed his head in shame.

'What could be worse than what you have already confessed?' Thomas answered fearfully.

The doctor sighed heavily as he wiped his brow with a handkerchief. 'I've also killed one,' he said sombrely.

Thomas's shock and initial silence spoke volumes as he sat agape and absorbed the doctor's reveal. Without sympathy, he went on to warn the doctor of the dangers of his secret mission to protect his patient. However, the doctor fully opened up and told him that the police had been asking questions over at the Royal College of Surgeons. And that a new inspector had been drafted in to find the culprit. The doctor told Thomas that all the surgeons in London were under suspicion, but like themselves, the new inspector was a Dorset man.

'Oh, but you're not a murderer, are you? You're a physician for heaven's sake. You've sworn the hippocratic oath. You're a saver of life.' Thomas endorsed his friend as a hero.

'I know. But I have a duty to protect my patient. Surely you can understand my reasons, Thomas,' the doctor shot back at him. Thomas put a consoling hand upon his shoulder and sucked on his pipe as they gazed through the window and down upon people toing and froing from one side of the street to to the other.

'If you're detained because of this patient of yours, it really wouldn't bear thinking about. You do realise this, don't you?' Thomas warned as he searched the doctor's eyes for clarity.

'Yes, of course' the doctor replied dismissively. 'I've been giving it a great deal of thought, believe you me.'

'Anyway, I've been meaning to tell you, I've been doing some research into the old society. I wanted to speak to you about its reinvention. It's a very old one that was set up to protect and acquaint businessmen here in London. It dates back to medieval England.

'Maybe you ought to start saving some of that blood, then. We might have to use it for our initiation,' Thomas joked.

'Yes! That's exactly what I was thinking, Thomas! But wait. The press agency has given Jack and I a hilarious sobriquet; They're calling us Jack the Ripper,' the doctor replied gleefully. Thomas reacted with amusement then roared with laughter as the doctor began to chuckle alongside him.

'Well, maybe they should be calling you Jack, and the Ripper. Ha!' Thomas boomed, before he downed the dregs of his port. 'I hope they're not going to refer to me like that when they see us out together.'

'I hope not too. I wouldn't want you dragged into my mess, Thomas.'

'Why ever not? I think I'm going to enjoy this little game of yours.'

'Between you and me, I wrote a letter. Now the police believe they're looking for a maniac quack, because he writes letters in his victim's blood.'

'Oh. Absolute genius. So, we have an on-going game, then?' Thomas asked with an eagerness present in his eyes.

'Yes, well... The press are the ones making a game of it, not I,' he replied curtly.

Thomas had finally succumbed to the doctor's involvement and began to understand why he had to protect his patient. If Jack was the demon who'd ripped up little Polly Nichols, it would have put the doctor in a very awkward position, especially with his high society friends and work colleagues.

'So, to Jack and the Ripper, then.' Thomas hailed with his empty glass in hand. 'And let us not forget all the Dorset Men here in London either. My word... this is looking better than my novel. Damn you, man.' Thomas remarked in jest before they recited another verse of the poem.

'"If you could zee their comely gaït,
An' pretty feäces' smiles,
A-trippèn on so light o' waïght,
An' steppèn off the stiles;
A-gwaïn to church, as bells do swing

An' ring 'ithin the tow'r,
You'd own the pretty maïdens' pleäce
Is Blackmwore by the Stour.'"

And with the doctor's confession now disclosed, all that was left to do was to get his patient's admission of guilt. And then the drunken whores would no longer be inspired to run amok upon the streets of Whitechapel. And the doctor's game would only end when Pearly Poll was found and brought to book. And the doctor hadn't felt better about finishing the job he was asked to do. In his mind failure to find her was no longer an option, and a secret society would add a cloak of steel to their circle and protect them from the authorities who were by now at sixes and sevens in their hunt to find the Ripper.

18

Jack carefully shaped his model of St. Philips Church, using the same knife he'd used to slice up Polly Anne Nichols in his nightmare. The doctor appeared from the bathroom and dried his hands on a towel. He passed Jack a knowing grin as he rolled his shirt sleeves down and began to button up his cuffs. Whilst in the bathroom he'd deliberated how he was going to coax his patient into a confirming his hand in the brutal murder of the whore, so he began with a generous acknowledgment of his patient's steady hand, while he observed him at work with his model. Jack hadn't much to do in his spare time and his artistry with his replication of the church opposite was living proof of his incredible knife skills, and the doctor studied him in admiration.

'Let me tell you something, Jack,' the doctor said brightly.

Jack continued to focus on his cardboard model before he turned to look at his doctor.

'What is it, Doctor?'

'I truly believe you would have made quite a decent surgeon had you put your mind to it,' he remarked as he folded the towel and stepped back inside the bathroom. Jack's eyes followed him as he did so.

'Do you really think so, Doctor? Jack spluttered as he lost focus and put down his knife.

'Absolutely. Why not indeed?' he heard his doctor reply from the bathroom.

'But I would never pass all those exams,' Jack replied, as the doctor entered the room again. He positioned himself by the mantelpiece and watched in awe his patient's forbearance.

'Of course you would, with a little help. You see, Jack, it's imperative that a surgeon has a steady hand, just like yours... as I've said to you many times before' The doctor began to remind him of the time he told him about the skills of a surgeon. Jack hadn't forgotten and was equal to his doctor's mind games. But he was very much enjoying their little chat. For the first time in his life he felt so wonderful and happy.

'Oh. You are too kind, Doctor. But I could never master the art of performing and operation,' Jack remarked, as he gazed at the church through the window.

'Yes. True. But I couldn't imagine myself being able to master what you are doing right there with your model, without a little helping hand. You see, Jack, what you possess is the first requirement of any surgeon in the land - a steady hand. Also, by the way you focus,' the doctor commented as he attempted to ingratiate his patient with numerous compliments. The doctor wanted to appear sincere, but his true intention was to worm his way into his patient's psyche, akin to a bed bug inside a mattress. He went on congratulating Jack throughout their verbal exchanges and Jack felt completely overwhelmed by his doctor's eulogising over his handiwork.

The doctor thought it might be a good idea if he told Jack about his own childhood experiences, and revealed just how he loved to look at the innards of small creatures, such as rabbits, squirrels and hares: He told Jack how he'd once opened up a badger with a pen knife when he was just a small boy. This made Jack feel very much at ease and he'd forgotten all about his attack on Polly Nichols, due to a reversion in his memory. The doctor was informed of this atavism in Jack's psyche from his psychoanalyst and colleague Dr. Tuckett. He'd explained to the doctor about Jack's relapse to his normal phenotype, during the second mutation, or return to his past state of mind.

'So how would you like to watch me perform an appendectomy in the hospital theatre?' the doctor asked him.

'Oh can I, Doctor?' Jack replied excitedly as he put down his knife and clapped his hands in elation. Jack always liked to clap his hands when he was elevated, or in high spirits.

'You shall.' The doctor imagined the thought of his patient standing inside the theatre as he performed surgery on an agonising patient about to be operated upon. And how might a patient react to someone sitting in a corner of the room whilst having their appendix removed? This thought made the doctor smile and chuckle inwardly.

'But then, who should we perform this operation upon, Jack?' the doctor asked as he began to question his patient's integrity. Dr. Tuckett was the real genius when it came to matters concerning the psyche. He thought about approaching Dr. Tuckett again, should he fail in securing a confession from his patient today.

'Oh. Oh. A wretched whore, Doctor. They're still coming to my window and trying to scare me when I am trying to sleep, especially weekends.' The doctor gritted his teeth and snarled when Jack divulged that to him, because he suspected this just added to the reason for his patient's loathing of them.

'I've already warned that night porter that you were not to be woken during the night. He obviously needs reminding. Don't you worry, Jack, I shall make sure I have another word with him when I leave.'

'Oh, no, no, you don't understand, Doctor. He is not here at all weekends.' Jack reminded him. 'These horrible people come to my window when they know he is not here.'

'I see,' the doctor replied as he buttoned up his shirt collar. 'Look, Jack, I have a confession of my own that I need to discuss with you,' the doctor told him. 'If you feel that I have let you down in any way, please do say so, won't you?' The doctor said as his eyes narrowed and became darker.

'I know you are busy with your work, Doctor?' Jack replied, aware that the doctor had something more sinister on his mind. In his own fractured mind the doctor could do no wrong. The doctor was his teacher. He trusted him with impunity and anything he disclosed would stay firmly locked away inside his mind.

The doctor went on to explain to his patient, his own sleepless nights and anxiety he was having to nurse since the death of the whore. The doctor explained when he'd spotted another whore called Annie Chapman during the early hours, on his way to work, and how she reminded him of his personal anguish, because he had become quite depressed that Jack would be blamed for Polly Nichols's murder, since she had been found so close to the hospital. And he had learned since, from the coroner that the knife used to cut her open was itself a blunt knife. And the smell of apricot upon her clothes, a clue to the person who'd attacked her, plus the red stains of blackberry juice found on her collar all pointed to his patient. He expressed just how he'd butchered Annie Chapman, because he felt forced to do so. And why he thought it necessary to surgically remove her organs after he examined what was left of Polly Nichols's carved up body as she laid upon a slab inside the greengrocer's shop, where Jack himself had once been exhibited for a shilling. The doctor went on to explain just how he fed the whore with blackberries, before disemboweling her in the dark with his surgical knife. And when he finally finished his confession to Jack, he sat upon the foot of the bed and asked him what he thought he should do?.

Jack stood quietly looking out of the window as he digested his doctor's excuses for murdering Annie Chapman. He knew now was the time to repent for his own sins, if any, to his doctor, and it would have a profound effect that would bring himself and his doctor into an everlasting friendship. But the doctor's gambit had faltered as he began to run out of patience with Jack's reluctance to confide in him.

'Look, I'm not going to beat about the bush any longer, Jack. I know it was you who did for Polly Nichols. That's why I felt compelled to do the other one. I killed her just to protect you, before they come marching over here with their torches aflame and their axes sharpened at the ready to chop off your head... and mine, come to think of it.' The doctor became angry, because of his patient's reticence concerning the murder. 'Christ, Jack. You need to wake up, like I have done for you.' The doctor's tolerance now wafer thin, since without a confession from his patient, the murder committed upon Annie Chapman would have all been in vain. And since killing her in the manner so savage, he had been driven to drinking absinth and dabbling in laudanum.

'Oh, I don't know,' he spluttered. 'There is a person in my nightmare.'

'Whose are you talking about, Jack?'

'A man. He has a knife. Oh, I'm really not sure. I don't know him.'

The doctor sighed in relief as he stood up and nodded his head in approval. 'I'm with you all the way, Jack. We're in this together now,' he assured him as he placed a hand lightly upon his shoulder.

'But I do repent each morning, Doctor. I try not to think about her. I only wanted to speak to her. I panicked. I was afraid. I am very sorry if I did something to her. I have been to the chapel everyday to pray for her soul. I am having the most terrible nightmares. I cannot sleep. I am a bird. Oh, I just want to sleep and never wake up.' A tear rolled down his cheek as he stared into the wall behind the doctor. 'I don't want to be like the daemon in the book any longer, Doctor. I cannot bear to open my eyes. Oh, can't you send me away now?' he pleaded with his doctor whilst in abject torment.

'Like *The Man in the Iron Mask,* is that what you want?'

'Yes, Doctor. Like the man in the mask.'

The doctor sighed a heavy heart. He believed he had finally gotten his patient's confession and felt relieved that he and his patient could stand together in the Ripper stakes, since they shared a ghastly secret they would carry with them to their graves. The doctor was convinced they had each drawn the blood from a whore. Now it would be someone else's turn, but next time in the name of the doctor's reinvented society.

'We have both repented for our sins now, Jack. And did you know the press agency has given us a sobriquet? They are calling us Jack the Ripper. A dear friend of mine reckons they should be calling us Jack, and the Ripper. That gave us real fits.'

Jack remained silent as he watched the doctor closely. He noticed his excitement at the events surrounding the murders. 'I promise you, Jack, you will not see one single whore within one hundred yards of this hospital after one o'clock in the morning by the time we've finished with them. If so, I'll be waiting for them when they do. And if they as much as show a whisker at your window, I will cut off their breasts and stuff them inside their filthy mouths. And I promise you, I will be doing this just for you. But first, there is a job to be done. Together we will rid Whitechapel of this immoral filth forevermore.'

Jack looked up at the doctor and knew he would always be safe as long as he had his doctor to protect him, because it was his insecurities that had haunted him in the past, and this had led to the activation of his vexation and exasperation. He also knew he would never want to turn back the clock, or return to his dark past. He'd thought about escaping from Whitechapel altogether, to find sanctuary elsewhere in the countryside. He knew he was capable, since he'd proved his survival skills before when he was in Belgium. He could hide in the dark like the daemon in the novel, *Frankenstein*. But he knew that his confession could lead to his own murder one day.

'You know, a dear friend of mine is in London right now. He is going to finish his novel whilst he is here. I thought we might go out together at the weekend. I thought we could go hunting for a whore.' the doctor remarked as he twiddled with his moustache. 'Well, what do you say, Jack? Are you fit for it? We're already damned, are we not? So let's play their little game and give them what they really desire... after all, this is what they crave, is it not?'

Jack remained silent as he continued to gaze out of the window.

'Oh, don't worry. No harm will come of it, I give you my word. And let's face it, Jack, nobody can hide in the dark like you can,' he remarked, now that he and Jack were a team. 'But first I want you to sit down and copy a letter I have written out,' he said as he picked up his Gladstone bag from the floor and took out a notepad and bottle of red stuff, along with a quill.

'Now, you just copy what is written on this notepad. And you must write it down, exactly word for word. As you see, I have added a touch of Dorset dialect just to confuse them.' Jack complied with the doctor's wishes, as he dipped the quill into the jar.

"From Hell

Mr Lusk

I send you half the kidne I took from one women prasarved it for you tother piece I fried and ate it was very nise I may send you the bloody knif that took it out if you only wate a whil longer.

Signed catch me when you can.

Mishter Lusk."

When Jack had finished with his handwritten version of the letter, the doctor picked it up and read it back to himself as his eyes darkened when he suffered uncontrollable fits of laughter that filled his patient's mind with fear.

'Excellent!' He was more than delighted with Jack's contribution to his little game with the press, which he proposed to send with a half of human kidney that he took from Annie Chapman, after he'd opened her up and surgically removed her organs.

Jack's handwriting was erratic, like that of a person who'd suffered from a neurological disease, and Jack had suffered from neurofibromatosis; a neurological disorder that accompanied his proteus syndrome.

It was after the doctor congratulated his patient that he slipped on his coat from behind the door, then set the letter inside his pocket. Jack stood mindful of every word he'd written down for the doctor. But he was positively excited. The reality of going hunting with the doctor was exhilarating for him, and hiding in the dark was as good as it could get when it came to playing hide and seek with his doctor.

19

The slayings of Martha Tabram, Polly Nichols, and now Annie Chapman had caused shockwaves and enmity among the folk living within the perimeters of the murderous square mile of Whitechapel, and questions were starting to be asked, and accusations a plentiful as to the perpetrator's true identity began to rifle out of control among the blamers. Everyone living in the vicinity were horrified by the horrific murders being carried out right under their very noses, though violence not unheard of, like the occasional garrotting of the unsuspecting stranger, or knife attack to befall any gang member should they have strolled off their own manor by mistake. The Old Nichol Gang were most feared, as were the Flower and Dean gang at Thrawl Street, who would often steal night takings from prostitutes, depending on how desperately hungry they were themselves.

However, a new detective inspector had been drafted in by the police commissioner, his job was *not* to find the murderer anytime soon. Though the inspector was thought to be a first class officer of the law, having worked for Scotland Yard at Whitehall, he was understood to be a drunk and opium user, so by choosing him, the top brass would be able to evade catching the killer anytime soon. The word among those who knew Detective Inspector George Abberline was that he was addicted to opium. Nevertheless, the inspector did have an in-depth knowledge of Whitechapel, having worked the boundaries earlier in his career when he was a police constable. DI George Abberline had projected himself through the ranks with a number of convictions upon his captures of murderers and thieves alike, and he was thought to be an honorable servant to Her Majesty. He was sent directly from Whitehall to Whitechapel upon her orders, and his duty was to notify Charles Warren on a daily basis, in regards to his progress with his search for the culprit known as Jack the Ripper. The jokers at the press agency had made the horrific murders into a game of cat and mouse. Their claim was that they were actively receiving letters from somebody identifying themself as Jack. But it was highly regarded by Inspector Abberline that these foolhardy journalist's had written the letters themselves to sell more newspapers and profit from the slayings. And because of this fact, the inspector felt that his job of catching the killer would be a difficult one.

Detective Inspector Abberline was an immaculately dressed man with gaunt facial features, thinning hair, and a neatly trimmed beard. His deep set eyes reflected his discretion and professionalism. His garb, a long black coat, black suit trousers, and black waistcoat housed a gold pocket watch that hung from a thin chain.

Inside The White Hart public house, Abberline placed his top hat down on a small round table as he and his sergeant sat down with their drinks. This drinking den was a claustrophobic little public house situated on the northside of the Whitechapel Road, adjacent to Gunthorpe Alley, and where Martha Tabram had been previously butchered and left in a pool of blood.

Sergeant Thomas Arnold was a tall, heavily built man that bore a wild and untrimmed ginger beard. His small lively eyes reflected an intolerance and a fervour to catch the culprit responsible for the recent murders. He was angry that another detective had been given the job of finding the Ripper, but was in awe of the inspector's success rate. He questioned Scotland Yard's integrity when he asked them why he had not been selected to lead the hunt to find the killer that was lurking within the perimeters of his patch, since he'd also been successful in securing convictions for murderers, as in the case of Israel Lipski; the Jew who had murdered a young pregnant woman inside a room at Batty Street last year. And Arnold also knew the area like the back of his hand, and was fearsome to local crime gangs who'd referred to him as the Giant. It was when Abberline read Thomas Arnold's file, he was intrigued to know more about the Lipski murder of Miriam Angel one year ago.

'Tell me about Israel Lipski, Sergeant. Did you really believe he was guilty as charged?' Abberline asked, before he poured a mouthful of gin down his throat. Abberline was fascinated by the case of Israel Lipski. It was said by those involved with the case that Lipski was a melancholic frail man, ill fated. The Home Office had taken some pity upon him, and had even considered his release, due to the unnatural circumstances surrounding the case. But as news of his heinous crime began to gather pace by way of the press, local folk began accusing and in some cases even assaulting anybody thought to be of Jewish lineage.

Thomas Arnold spoke in a croaky cockney accent and was convinced that the right man had been convicted and hung for her murder.

'That poor woman's murder certainly left its mark around these parts,' Arnold replied, deep agitation in his voice as he leant across the table and stared coldly into the inspector's eyes. He continued to educate the inspector with some gruesome facts concerning the Lipski trial. And Abberline listened with interest. 'The problem was that Lipski's version of events never held up in court. He reckoned he was robbed by two of his employees, before they forced him to swallow that nitric acid… along with that young woman.'

'Did they find these employees of his?' Abberline inquired further.

'Nah, did they hell... not once they got whiff we were looking for 'em. They buggered off to another area. We searched the whole place for 'em. We couldn't find hide nor hare of 'em,' Arnold replied in angst.

'What was the name of this young woman, again?'

'Miriam Angel. And that she was, according to her husband,' the sergeant replied, before the rest of his cider hit the back of his throat. 'There were traces of aqua fortis on Lipski's coat, so we knew it was him that did it… No doubt in my bloody mind it was him.' Arnold was adamant that they had hung the right man and told Abberline about the anger that over-spilled onto the streets from the Lipski case, and how it had caused huge disharmony between Jews and Christians living together. Jewish community leaders had complained on several occasions to the police about the beatings and name calling, "Jewish murderer," whenever a death occurred in Whitechapel.

'Why'd he kill her, d'you think?' Abberline asked.

'That's easy to answer; to rob her, that's why. He'd planned to impose himself upon her, even though she was six months pregnant, Arnold replied bitterly. 'A murdering Jew is what he was, Inspector. We got the right man, all right. I'm as certain as I'm sitting here talking to you now.'

Detective Inspector Abberline was not so sure that Israel Lipski was in actual fact the killer of Miriam Angel, and he resented Thomas Arnold for not finding the other two men who had worked for Lipski at the time, and who Lipski had claimed were the real murderers.

'Was she married?' Abberline asked.

'Oh yeah, she was married, all right. Isaac Angel's, husband's name. A Jewish migrant from Hungary, I believe We later found that out when he appeared in court.'

'So what happened to him after her death, did he return to Hungary?' Abberline asked.

'Did he hell! No, he went back to the address and attempted to murder the landlady, that's what he did… all because she bore the same surname as Lipski.'

'How'd you mean?'

'How do I mean what, Inspector?'

'Yes how did he try to murder her, Sergeant?'

'Oh, that. Well he went back to the building with two of his relatives and kicked her half to death, that's what he did.'

'Where did he kick her, exactly?'

'About the abdomen mainly. Apparently she almost died of her injuries, so I heard.'

'Was he sent down?'

'Nah, he wasn't. He was bound over to keep the peace for one year.'

'And where is he now? Did you keep a watchful eye on him?'

'Nah, not really. I have no idea where he could be, Inspector.'

'Try and find him, will you? I'd like to have a few words with him, that's if he's still in the area.'

'I'll make enquiries at once.'

'Good heaven's. Poor chap. You never know what a man might be capable of after finding his wife and unborn murdered like that.'
Abberline believed if the motive regarding the recent murders was revenge, then Isaac Angel would certainly have a reason to be so revengeful. He'd recalled reading in the journals over the past year, paragraphs concerning random attacks on such women as Annie Millwood from Whites Row in Spitalfields, who was stabbed in the abdomen by a complete stranger for no apparent reason. She later died from her injuries,

after returning to work. 'What kind of person do you think would murder in such a manner as the Ripper, then, Sergeant?'

'A bloodthirsty ghoul like creature, I would say, Inspector. A bloodthirsty ghoul. Only a perfect savage would commit such a crime on defenseless women, such as the Nichols and Chapman women,' Arnold replied bitterly.

'So in your opinion, Sergeant, would you say that we are looking for more than one killer?'

'Nah. The same hand killed them all is my guess,' Arnold suggested.

But Abberline's other angle was they might be looking for a surgical hand in the case of Chapman, and so he planned to speak to some of the surgeons at the local charity hospital; particularly as the disembowelment of Annie Chapman bore alternative clues to that of Polly Nichols, and Marta Tabram. In Abberline's mind, Annie Chapman's killer was a master surgeon, since the incisions inflicted upon her body were clearly defined by a steady hand, and the removal of her organs in the pitch black suggested the person who'd sliced her up knew his trade. And the first doctor to examine her, clearly stated that she was murdered by someone with years of surgical experience, unlike the attack upon Polly Nichols, Annie Chapman was murdered by a skilful right handed person who had used a sharp surgical knife, as opposed to a left handed killer who had used a blunt knife. Abberline contemplated the dichotomy with those two murders. But he was confident the killer had an obsession with the abdomen and the sexual organs, which could reflect the loss of a child at birth.

And as the two of them discussed past and recent murders, an argument broke out between a group of four elderly men sitting behind them. They were heard discussing the Ripper murders and a disagreement soon erupted about who the culprit might be.

'Ah! Get off y'self! Only a beast would have murdered these women in such a disgusting way as that!' one of the scruffy looking carmen shouted from across the table.

'The only beasts round 'ere are Jews!' another shot back with a sharp tongue.

'Personally, I'd like to see the back of the lot of 'em,' a third man replied in resentful fervour.

At that point a chagrined Abberline stood up from the table and approached the bar with his sergeant rushing to keep up. Abberline placed his bag down on the counter and opened it. He took out a wine glass wrapped in brown paper. He showed the wine glass to the tall bearded barman, then asked if he could recall if the wine glass may have been taken from his establishment on the night Polly Nichols was murdered? The barman told Abberline that it was certainly possible, since customers did often leave and return with their glasses at a later hour, or even the next day. Abberline thanked the barman for his assistance, then told him to be watchful for any person he suspected of being a lunatic.

'The way I see it, Inspector, is these women round 'ere are asking for trouble, they are. I mean, falling about drunk and showing themselves off like they do. There ought to be a bleedin' law against it or summink. These women… you know what I'm saying, Inspector?' the barman remarked as the inspector and his sergeant turned to leave.

'Yes. You are doubtless,' Abberline replied in agreement. He grabbed his top hat from the sergeant as they exited the pub.

'Come on, Arnold. Let's get ourselves over to Leman Street and have a little chat with Leather Apron. Let's see what he's got to say for himself. Though I doubt if he murdered Annie Chapman… unless he's a Quack… and he's been hiding it from everyone,' Abberline remarked sardonically.

On the busy street it was a glorious sunny day and people were on the move. Abberline and Arnold stopped in their tracks and observed a two horse carriage came hurtling through the street. It bore a name written in large gold letters, *Great Eastern Railways.* A crowd tried desperately to look at the victim lying inside the carriage. And as they crossed the busy Whitechapel Road, Abberline considered the task in catching a madman on the loose. A volatile community would be ready to blame anyone as long as he was a Jew. John Piza, who was also known as Leather Apron found this out quickly to his despair upon his immediate arrest. He was seized for the murder of Annie Chapman, because he had beaten and thrashed his wife on the morning of her murder. Anti-Semitism was widespread and Jewish men were now referred to as, "Lipski;" the pseudonym, for Jewish murderer.

20

The doctor sat at a small desk, behind the entrance door to a small room on the second floor of a tenement block at Batty, a side street located south off Commercial Road at Aldgate. A sash cord window to his left looked directly down upon the busy thoroughfare, and an oil lamp aflame emitted just enough heat and light as to read his own handwriting. The room was sparsely furnished, except for a disused bookcase at the far end. A single wrought iron bed, a wardrobe and a chest of drawers furnished the bedroom perpendicular. A sink basin was stationed beneath a window that looked out across the rooftops and backyards of dwellings to the rear.

Thomas sat quietly as he focused his eyes on a journal as he smoked his clay pipe.

The doctor had written copies of a letter that he intended to send to all the Dorset men that he knew were living in and around London, since he expected they should be interested in bonding with his reinvented society. Such people included barrister Montague John Druitt; He lived and worked at London Temple Inns of Court. The doctor was well acquainted with his father, who was also a surgeon like himself, and most importantly a Dorset man. He had also included Dorset architect G.R Crickmay. Once upon a time Thomas had worked for G.R Crickmay's architects as a junior assistant, though he wasn't quite a Dorset man in London just yet. G.R Crickmay was looking to expand his business in London's east end ,and Spitalfields was one such area that had taken his interest. An opportunity had arisen to purchase some land had come to his attention, so he was very keen to make a bid for this prime real-estate within Spitalfields and

Whitechapel. He'd had it on good source that the price per square foot had dropped considerably since the murder of Annie Chapman at Hanbury, so there was a killing to be made which would have benefited Crickmay substantially. And with the professional services of Montague, John Druitt, purchasing Spitalfields would be snapped up at a pittance. The doctor knew, with Montague, John Druitt, and G.R Crickmay on board it would add yet another ring of steel to his secret society, should it come to fruition before the end of the term.

***

Detective Inspector Abberline and Sergeant Thomas Arnold waited patiently to cross the busy Commercial Road at the junction with Settles Street. The noisy clatter from horse drawn carriages and wheelbarrows being hurried along seemed to annoy him somewhat, as he cursed and attempted to shoo them out of his way for straying of course, and coming too close to the pavement. People toing and froing and milling around made the whole area feel congested. And when they'd finally managed to cross the busy thoroughfare, they immediately walked down Batty with a purpose, until they stopped at a block on the west side of the street. The inspector gazed up at the number sixteen stamped on the door, before he and Arnold entered the dimly lit building. They squeezed themselves up the creaking narrow staircase, besieged by dry rot, and stopped outside a door, signified by the letter C. The inspector tapped his knuckles twice upon the door and stepped back as he awaited an answer.

Inside the dimly lit room, the sound of the knock had caused the doctor, and Thomas to look up in surprise, before they gazed at one another in anticipation and what they should do about it. The doctor quietly climbed to his feet and stood at the table, as Thomas shook his head in wonder. The doctor put his finger to his lips to hush Thomas's attempts to utter a sound, before he slid the letter into the open drawer and gently closed it shut. Thomas put down his journal and showed the doctor a knowing expression, then climbed to his feet.

'Who the hell could that be?' Thomas whispered as he quietly stepped towards the door.

The doctor shook his head. 'I have no idea,' he quietly replied as he stepped over and put an ear to the door frame.

'Well, answer it. See who it is, for heaven's sake,' Thomas suggested with an eagerness of an excited puppy.

'Yes, I will, then.' The doctor waited a moment as he queried his own judgement, before he opened the door to the inspector and his sergeant.

'Yes? What can I do for you?' the doctor asked irksomely.

Abberline engaged him with a smile, then respectfully put out an outstretched hand. 'Good evening to you, Sir' the inspector replied warmly.

'What is it?' the doctor asked abruptly as he sighed in annoyance at them standing there like they were selling something.

'I'm Detective Inspector Abberline of Scotland Yard,' he replied, before he turned to his sergeant. 'And this is Sergeant Arnold,' he went on. 'May we have a word?' he asked as he took the liberty of putting a foot forward inside the opened door.

'Yes, of course. How rude of me. Come in, do,' the doctor replied, as he stepped aside and let them through. He could feel his chest tightening, because of this unexpected visit by an inspector and an angry looking sergeant. And as they followed him inside the room, he wondered if he might already be a suspect in the hunt for the Ripper. The murder of Annie Chapman flashed through his mind, step by step, in case he may have left anything incriminating by her cadaver. Maybe he left something at the scene of her murder? He wondered if they had spoken to his patient before calling upon himself.

He quietly closed the door shut behind them as they stood stiffly, purposeful as they scanned the room. Thomas had stationed himself by an old disused bookcase at the far end, his journal in hand as he sucked on his pipe.

'So how can we be of any help to you, Inspector?' the doctor asked compliantly, as he glanced over his shoulder at Thomas. But Detective Inspector Abberline immediately recognised Thomas with a friendly acknowledgement. He was an avid reader of Thomas's books. He had read them all, and so stood in awe when he spotted him observing them with a keen eye.

'Let me introduce ourselves to you. I'm chief surgeon at the London Hospital,' he said courteously. 'And as you're probably aware, this is my good friend Thomas. He has travelled all the way from Dorset to be here.'

'Good heavens. I recognised you immediately,' Abberline replied heartily. 'I'm one of your biggest admirers, Sir.'

'Well, he is here seeking inspiration for his forthcoming novel,' the doctor disclosed, before Abberline focused his eyes upon him.

'And I've seen your picture in The Times journal, regarding the Elephant Man,' Abberline replied as he caught the doctor's icy gaze back at him. 'Let me applaud you for all you have done in finding him a permanent home. It couldn't have been easy for either of you.'

'Quite right,' the doctor replied. 'Quite frankly, it's been a dolorosa.'

Abberline stepped towards Thomas with an outstretched hand. 'It's a pleasure to meet you,' he said warmly 'I'm a huge supporter of Dorset writers.'

'That's very decent of you, old boy,' Thomas replied respectfully as he shook the inspector's hand.

'So it's business and pleasure, then?' Abberline retorted.

'Yes it is,' Thomas replied. 'The doctor and I are on a mission to connect as many London street names with that in Dorset. Are you a Dorset man yourself, Inspector?' Thomas boldly asked.

'Blandford Forum, actually.'

'By the Stour?' the doctor remarked.

'That's correct,' Abberline confirmed his geography.

'So we're all Dorset men here, then?' Thomas remarked jovially. 'How Wonderful.'

'If you pardon the exception of my good self,' Arnold interjected as he cleared his throat.

'That's all right, old boy, we can't all be Dorsetonians, can we?' Thomas replied.

'Say, maybe you'll be interested in joining our society, then, Inspector?' Thomas suggested with an added optimism.

'What society would that be?' Abberline asked.

'A society that only involves Dorset men. Have you heard of us?' the doctor asked.

He knew it would add another ring of steel, should the inspector become a fully fledged member.

'What kind of society are we talking about?' the inspector enquired. 'Like the Freemasons, is it?'

'Something like that, yes,' Thomas intervened, before he poked his mouth with his pipe.

'Just as well.' The inspector Abberline was a cautious man. He could sense something quite surreal going on under his nose, and the attention he might receive in regards to joining a society of this nature.

'Well, you'd be very welcome to join us, Inspector,' the doctor reminded him. He knew this unexpected meeting may turn out to be in his favour after all.

'To be completely honest with you, I'm not really the society type of person. But I will certainly give it some thought,' the Inspector replied. 'In fact, the reason I'm here is to see for myself where Miriam Angel was murdered. Israel Lipski murdered her in this room.

'Oh really? I wasn't aware,' the doctor replied in earnest.

'Not sure we can help you there, old chap,' Thomas piped up.

'I wouldn't know if you're aware, but this room was once occupied by her and her husband, Isaac Angel,' Abberline stated.

'Actually, I do recall reading something of that nature concerning a murder in Batty Street last year. As I recall Lipski was indeed hung for her murder.' the doctor replied with some knowledge of the case.

'Yes, quite. He was hung on August 22nd of last year, in fact. She was heavily pregnant when he killed her. I thought I might take a peek at her surroundings. Did you know he poured nitric acid down her throat before he forced himself upon her?' the inspector said, using a sombre tone of voice. He appeared anxious and needed to know where her despairing husband had disappeared to, since he had left without a trace, and there had been a spate of vicious attacks upon unsuspecting women in the past year that had regretfully gotten more violent. The inspector had a strong notion that Isaac Angel might be the person behind the deaths of at least two prostitutes murdered in Whitechapel, particularly as Isaac was bound over to keep the peace for one year since the end of August last, and that year by definition had expired since his court appearance.

'Does this mean you are considering a link between this woman's death and The Ripper murders?' Thomas asked with incredulity.

'I'm certainly not ruling anything out, though there are two other suspects we're trying to trace. They're still at large. They were employed by Lipski at the time of her murder. They absconded after Lipski was arrested. The recent murders could well be connected if we are to assume the attacks upon his victims abdominal area is the focus for these types of murders.' The inspector was a highly intelligent man with a vivid imagination, due to his drink and drug addiction, but the doctor approved of his hypothesis concerning these latest murders. 'Would you like us to leave the room, Inspector, whilst you take a look around?' the doctor asked.

'No, it's all right.' The inspector walked into the bedroom and they followed. Sergeant Arnold walked towards the window. The inspector stood next to him as he peered out at the surrounding dwellings. He pointed up at a window that looked straight down upon his position.

'There,' he said. 'Lipski's view of this room from his rear window. He must have been watching her before he made up his mind to force himself upon her. My sergeant found him cowering under her bed when he and his colleagues arrived here.'

'That's truly fascinating,' Thomas exclaimed as he stepped towards the window and looked up at where Lipski would have been spying her, as she washed herself down at the sink basin. The doctor checked his watch. 'I think I better get going, I have an appointment at Lincoln's Inn Fields with Sir. William Gull. I don't want to be late.'

'We'll be leaving anyway. I've seen what I came here to see. I want to look at all the rooms in this block today.' The inspector needed to see the view from one flat in particular and that was the flat that was let to Israel Lipski.

'Good,' the doctor replied, before he handed a business card to the Inspector Abberline. 'That's my card. If I can help you with anything, you'll find me over at the London Hospital.'

'Very well. Thank you, Doctor.' He slipped the card into his wallet. 'I could certainly do with your expertise concerning these murders,' the inspector said upon his exit.

'It'll be a pleasure to assist you wherever I can,' the doctor told him with a devious intention in his eyes.

The inspector and his sergeant stepped outside the door and turned to face the doctor.

'Oh yes. I almost forgot to ask you, how is that patient of yours coping these days?'

'You mean Jack. He's very well, thank you.'

'Yes, that's it. I couldn't remember his christian name. Elephant Man, I remember he was called.'

'He's doing very well since you ask. Would you like to meet him?'

'Maybe... when I can find the time. Give him my regards, won't you? You've done a fine job with him, so I hear.'

The doctor acknowledged the inspector's tribute, before he closed the door shut behind them.

'"The Juwes are the men that will be blamed for nothing?"' the doctor muttered as he stepped back inside the room.

'You sure about that, old boy?' Thomas asked as he took his seat.

The doctor showed him a look of defiance as he gritted his teeth and his eyes turned to black. 'The night is very young, Thomas, and there is a job to be done,' he exclaimed.

21

Catherine Eddowes fell down in yet another drunken stupor as she attempted to scurry along the pavement. She had become a constant nuisance to both the passing traffic and the general public. A horse drawn carriage reared up in front of her as she stepped carelessly into the middle of the road. She leant backwards and waved her fist angrily at the cab driver as he screamed for her to get out of his way. But she had been chancing her luck all afternoon and quite deliberately sat herself down in front of the oncoming traffic. By way of her actions she was asking to be ridden over. She had wanted to end her life and leave a world where only hardship and beatings had become a way of life for the likes of her unfortunate self. The truth was that she was in despair, because of her failure to return home to her violent partner with her night takings. The reason she hadn't done so, was because she had spent all her income on alcohol, and she knew she was going to get another beating from him, so instead she had decided to get herself arrested so she could spend the rest of the day inside a cell at the local police station, at least until her return to sobriety. She had shared an accommodation with a brutal bigot who'd forced upon her to feed and water him at regular intervals. But she had been out drinking until the early hours, between selling herself for whatever she could make.

A local beat officer soon spotted a crowd gathering around her as he laid down at the corner by Aldgate Pump. He hurried towards her and grabbed her by the arm as she screamed blue murder and attempted to shrug him off. But he'd managed to drag her along the ground by the scruff and back onto the safety of the pavement, where a local butcher stood at a barrow gutting a dead rabbit. He discarded the creature's innards into an empty wooden box as she furiously yelled abuse at him.

'Murderer! Bloody Murderer, you are! You should be the one gutted y'self! You 'orrible man!'

'And clean that mess up!' the officer warned him as he was forced to step aside from the bloodied mess on the filthy pavement.

'I will… once I've skinned her proper!' the hairy butcher fired back at him as he slung the carcass over his forearm, like he'd done so a thousand times before.

'Get off me, you bloody git! Just leave us alone! I wasn't 'urtin' nobody, was I?!' she screamed at the officer as he pinned her to a wall at the side of the road, and held tightly her arms behind her back.

'You're drunk and disorderly. You're coming with me, madam,' he yelled back at her.

'And what are you looking at?' she yelled as she turned her head to look at a passing stranger when he stopped and shook his head at her in disgust. She stared back at him as the fleas danced upon his heavily matted beard, and a sewer rat popped its head out of his jacket pocket while he stood grinning at her, like a lunatic who'd just escaped the hothouse.

The officer was joined by another constable and together they marched her off towards Bishopsgate Police Station, as she screamed obscenities at those who dared to make eye contact with her.

22

Inside the receiving room the doctor worked tirelessly, attending to sick patients when a hysterical young woman rushed towards him whilst clutching a baby. The child was wrapped in a soiled sheet. He spotted her immediately so climbed to his feet to give her his full attention. She handed him the child.

'What the hell has happened?' he asked using an austere tone of voice as he looked down at the infant.

'Oh, Doctor, please help me,' she cried. 'I turned me head for one bleedin' minnit before he screamed. His clothes were on fire.'

With deep concern the doctor lifted up the sheet with his forefinger to look at the baby's injuries. 'I can see that,' he barked at her as he looked closely into the baby's blank eyes and felt for a pulse. 'But why have you brought your baby to the receiving room? Your child is clearly dead. He is not breathing. He has no pulse.' He signalled to a nurse.

'No but you're mistaken, Doctor... he is breathing. Look for yourself,' she cried as she stood trembling wearing a bloodstained apron over a brown frilly dress. Her eyes pink and filled with tears, and her cheeks suffused with colour.

The doctor looked up and sighed while the nurse checked for life as she felt his limp hand.

'He is not,' the doctor dismissed her observation. 'My nurse will take your dead baby away. Now listen to me when I tell you your baby is dead.' The nurse confirmed this to the woman with a nod of the head. 'Now go with her and fill out a form concerning what happened to your baby.'

'But what am I gonna tell the ol' man? He'll bleedin' kill me when I tell him what's happened. He'll say I never looked after him proper. What am I gonna do, Doctor? What the hell am I s'posed to say to him?' she screamed in panic of her husband's temper.

'I'm sorry but that is not my concern right now. I am busy seeing others.' He replied before he marched off towards the long line of people waiting to be assessed and she was ushered away by the young sympathetic nurse.

'I turned round and the oil lamp was on top of him, it was, I swear. Oh, what am I to do?' she was led away saying.

And as the doctor looked across the room he spotted Detective Inspector Abberline standing inside the door with his hat in hand and a deep frown upon his pallid face. The room filled with the noise of the woman screaming in the background. 'Call yerself a doctor?! Some bleedin' help you are!'

Abberline approached the doctor with a raised brow. 'I see you have your hands full. What's wrong with that one?' he asked civilly.

'She has a dead baby. She thinks the poor child is still breathing.' The doctor paused for a moment. 'Anyway, what can I do for you, Inspector Abberline, so I remember? he replied, seemingly put out.

'We believe the Ripper may be a doctor of some kind. Maybe a quack, or possibly a surgeon.'

'Is he indeed?' The doctor replied knowingly as he attended to a patient suffering from a rash to the skin.

'Yes. It seems the killer's knowledge of the anatomy has been ascertained,' he said as he watched the doctor lift up his patient's pullover and put his stethoscope to his chest.

'Is that so?'

'It is so. Look, I am here to ask for your professional opinion. I have spoken to some of the other surgeons in the vicinity and they tell me that you are the go-to man as you are well acquainted to most, if not all of London's top surgeons. And you teach anatomy over at Queens Mary's medical centre.'

'True, but I'm not really qualified to pass judgement upon who your Ripper might be, Inspector.'

'Do you know of any medical person who may have an axe to grind with these whores?'

'Of course not. Have you not heard of the hippocratic oath?'

'Yes, I have, but nevertheless I am certain we are looking for a person of great anatomical knowledge. Annie Chapman's disembowelment is proof of that, according to the coroner's report. An expert in his field of surgery, it has been said.'

'I'm sorry but I am far too busy in here to take a swipe at any such person that I am supposed to imagine to be the Ripper, Inspector.'

'Fine. I am very sorry to have interrupted your session in the receiving room.' Abberline said as he turned to leave.

'If I hear of any such person, I will be in touch,' the doctor replied as Abberline turned to leave.

'That would be greatly appreciated,' Abberline turned back and uttered.

'Have you thought about joining our society yet?' The doctor reminded him with a faint smile.

'Yes, I have actually. I'll be in touch,' he replied as he opened the door.

'Excellent!' the doctor replied gleefully, before the detective inspector left without further ado.

23

Above the greengrocers shop Jack's bird of prey flew off from its eyrie and hovered uninhibitedly above the rooftops, beneath a coruscating night sky. He spotted the clock at the brewery when it struck midnight as he dropped his oversized blackberries upon the Commercial Street, while people dashed from one side of the thoroughfare to the other. And as always they scramble among themselves for the deadly fruit that hits the ground at lightning speed, then explode into tiny segments that cover their faces in that thick red goo, a reminder of Jack's recurring bloody visual upon each occasion he closed his eyes.

Prostitute, Long Liz stood by the entrance door to the White Hart public house and embraced a heavily bearded man. Her client's attire; a long grey coat that housed a black velvet collar. And he wore a flat cap. He ushered her by the waist into Gunthorpe Alley while he attempted to kiss her ear. She was quite drunk and when they'd reached a high wall, the client lifted her dress above her waist and slipped his penis inside her. And within a minute of humping her from behind, he'd reached his conclusion at the price of a sixpence.

And as she pulled up her bloomers, her client told her that he was satisfied, before he put himself away and stumbled off towards Osborne, a very happy chappie.

Elizabeth Stride made her way back to the White Hart and was about to enter the drinking den when she was accosted by Thomas as he tipped his hat and smiled at her warmly.

'Oh, ullo,' she said as she reciprocated his smile.

'Would you be willing to come with me?' he asked.

'Of course I would, but it'll cost ya,' she replied.

From across the road the doctor monitored them. He watched with interest as Thomas used his persuasive skills to lure her towards Berner Street, as she straightened her clothes and made herself tidy.

'How much would it cost for my friend and I to indulge you?' he asked, trying not to appear forceful, or crude.

'A shilling each, cos I can tell you're not from 'round these parts, are you?'

'Quite right. We're from the west country, my friend and I,' he replied as they crossed the thoroughfare towards Commercial Road.

The doctor bided his time as he waited at the junction with Berner as the bird of prey hovered high above his head.

On this occasion the doctor wore a brown jacket, red necktie, and a double peaked cap. Being a keen sailor, he would sometimes choose to wear a sailors attire. Sailing around the British Isles was often a way to spend part of his summer holidays. But tonight the doctor and his friend were high on absinth and laudanum, and he was very excited about the job that had been entrusted upon him to find Pearly Poll. And he was out to kill two birds with one stone as promised in a letter he had written to the press agency.

Long Liz stood at 5'5, and was of Swedish heritage. Her long, brown curly hair made her look extremely attractive in the darkness of the night. Her garb; a black jacket with fur trim at the collar, and a black dress and black bonnet taboot. A couple of years previous, she'd run her own coffee shop in the vicinity of Poplar, until her drinking had gotten the better of her and she began selling herself.

But the doctor was becoming increasingly edgy and checked his watch, as they approached arm in arm, as they bore happy facial expressions.

'Well, here he is,' Thomas told her playfully as the doctor stood expectantly.

Long Liz gazed up at the tall doctor and smiled as he ushered her down Berner Street on the south side of Commercial Road. The bird of prey had by now hidden himself in the dark corner inside Duffield's Yard by Berner.

'I'm going to have you in a place where we shall not be seen. Come this way, pretty maiden?' the doctor said to her, before he stopped in his tracks and quite chivalrously pinned a red rose containing a white maiden fern into the lapel of her woolen jacket.

'You are a gentleman,' she remarked as she acknowledged his chivalry.

'I'll just wait across the road. Give a shout when you're done and I'll come for my turn,' Thomas said as he parted company and left them standing outside Duffield's Yard. He'd agreed to keep watch, so disappeared out of sight.

But the doctor needed to ask her a question concerning that particular whore that he'd been instructed to find.

'Do you know of a woman who goes by the name Pearly Poll?' he asked her as he searched her eyes for clarity. Finding Pearly Poll was of paramount importance to furthering his career, and if he could locate her whereabouts tonight it would be an added bonus for him personally.

'No, I've never heard of her. Who is she?' she replied with a certain unease as she stared at the doctor in dismay.

'She's a whore... just like you, except she has an Irish accent,' the doctor responded with a menacing look upon his face as he towered over her small frame.

'Well, I've never heard of her. And I know most of the girls 'round 'ere, love. And just in case you get any ideas that I'm her, my name's Elizabeth Stride, you know.'

'That's fine, Lizzy. You'll do for now.'

And as the doctor pushed her into the yard, she gasped, while across the street, under a dimly lit street lamp, Thomas kept watch as he smoked his pipe. He wore his deerstalker and a tweed cape, bearing a resemblance to Sherlock Holmes, and in touching distance as to hear the argument b'twixt the doctor and a very frightened Long Liz.

'All right, but I thought of you and your friend,' she replied agitatedly, perturbed and confused by the disappearance of Thomas as she wrapped her curls around her forefinger.

'To be honest that was not the friend I had in mind,' the doctor replied, as she gazed into his daring black eyes.

'Then who?' she asked as she showed her concern.

'My friend Jack shall keep you busy for a while,' he went on to say as he looked down at her large breasts.

'Who's Jack?' Long Liz stood oblivious to what was about to befall her as she stood vulnerable inside the yard. She'd hoped her chance encounter would be worth more than just a shilling. It wasn't often two gentlemen would require her services at the same time.

'He is with us here.' the doctor replied. His excitement began to make him tremble as he fixed his eyes firmly upon her neck.

'You'll have to pay handsomely. I don't usually go for two, one after the other. It's only because you're such gentlemen, I'll manage it,' she answered as she steered her chest towards him.

'Call your friend, then,' she said, as she stroked his firm chest.

Thomas had disappeared from view as a passer-by engaged them from his position across the street.

'LIZZY!' the passer-by called out, because he knew her and believed she was in grave danger as the doctor viciously grabbed her throat.

'Hey! You! Come here!' Thomas came up behind the passer-by and chased after him.

In his panic, the doctor mounted his bicycle and quickly rode off towards Aldgate Pump. as Long Liz stood confused and unaware of her fate, before a hand appeared from behind her and sliced her throat from ear to ear. She murmured her demise, then fell to the ground inside the entrance to the yard, as the sound of horse clatter approaching began to intensify. Upon reaching the entrance to the yard the cart horse reared its head in sheer panic as Long Liz's body lay upon the ground with her throat severely cut - She was dead.

The panicked driver hurriedly jumped off his cart to see what had distracted his animal so much so. And when he spotted the whore lying still upon the ground, he cried out in horror.

"MURDER! MURDER! MURDER! MURDER!" he cried as he ran to fetch help.

24

At Bishopsgate Police Station, Catherine Eddowes stood soberly at the station sergeant's counter about to be released with a charge sheet.

'Name?' he asked as he stared at her with his cold blue eyes.

'What'd ya bleedin' think it is, then?' she replied as she attempted to hold herself together.

'If I thought anything, madam, I wouldn't be blimmin' well asking now, would I?' he fired back at her angrily.

'All,right! All right! Keep your bleedin' hair on, wontcha?' she screamed back at him.

'Look, madam, if you don't tell me your name, you'll be going straight back to that cell you just walked out of. Now what is it?' The station officer was losing his patience, but she wasn't bothered anyhow, because she knew that when she arrived home, she would be thrashed for getting herself arrested.

'Mary Kelly,' she replied with a raised brow as she looked at him questionably. Mary Kelly was an adopted pseudonym taken by the local prostitutes and used when they were arrested for being drunk and disorderly. This idea often meant they could get away with it.

So the station sergeant stepped out from around the counter and opened the door for her, before he grabbed her roughly by the arm and pushed her onto the dimly lit street.

'And don't let me catch you in here again!' he warned her as he slammed the door shut behind him.

Catherine Eddows looked up at the clouds in the night sky and screamed back at the station sergeant.

'Oh don't you worry, git face! You won't be seeing me ever again!' She straightened her black and green bonnet, then climbed to her feet and stumbled off towards Houndsditch, in the direction of Aldgate Pump, all the while she kept her eyes peeled for a customer as she searched the empty streets in vain. She knew if she could take home some money it may dissuade her partner from beating her and kicking her out on the street again.

***

Meanwhile, at Berner Street, Elizabeth Stride laid dead inside Duffield's Yard with her throat cut as a cacophony of police whistles rang out amid the panic. The fear among local residents was evident as a large crowd gathered outside the yard to look at her horrific injury. After chasing off the onlooker, Thomas had returned to his lodgings at Batty Street, whilst the bird of prey flew back towards his eyrie above the greengrocers shop.

And as he looked down upon the aftermath of her murder in Whitechapel, he spotted the doctor's long legs astride his bicycle and heading towards Houndsditch. He pecked wildly at his own chest, then began to track the doctor's movements. He looked down and watched as his doctor climbed off his bicycle in Goulston and leant it against the wall. And when the bird of prey hid himself in a dark shadow, he watched as the doctor took out a piece of chalk from his pocket and wrote across on the wall: "The Juwes are the men that will be blamed for nothing."

In Mitre Square by Houndsditch, Catherine Eddows had found a customer. She began to have sex with the bearded stranger up against the wall. Within a moment it was over and he dropped some coins to the floor before he went on his way.

The bird of prey landed on a rooftop that overlooked the square and watched her tidying herself, as she straightened her dress, then reset her bonnet. She was over her drunken period from earlier that day, and she was ready to return home, now that she had a shilling to offer her partner for her lodgings.

But the doctor had made a promise to the Central News Agency. And with that promise he'd stated that two whores would have to die tonight, so he knew that she would have to be killed also.

And after the stranger had vacated the square, Catherine cut a lonely figure as she stood with her back against the wall. She noticed a dark shadow heading towards her. It was a silhouette that showed the outline of the doctor as he approached, and he was ready to commit a dire deed upon her flesh.

'Who's that?' she asked afeard as the doctor stood over her with his sparkling knife in hand. He forcibly covered her mouth with his hand.

'A question for you,' he whispered as she nodded, stricken and trembling at the thought of his knife going into her abdomen.

'Your name... what is it?'

'Catherine... Catherine Eddows,' she whimpered, after he gently lifted his hand from her mouth so she could answer his question.

'Where can I find Pearly Poll? And don't lie, or I shall cut off your breasts.'

'Over at Mitre Court,' she replied in fear for her life.

'Mitre Court, you say?'

She nodded to confirm as her eyes bulged over his hand.

'And where is that, exactly?'

'Next to the doss houses,' she replied.

'Are you sure?'

'Yes, I swear, that's where she is,' she replied as the tears began to stream down her face. 'She calls herself Mary Jane Kelly,' she continued to say.

'Mary Jane Kelly?'

'Hm hm. Hm hm,' she mumbled as her tongue got tired.

'You did well,' he remarked calmly. 'But now you must die like the others.'

And before she had a chance to scream, she gasped as she took her last breath and slid down the wall, as the bird of prey appeared beside her cadaver.

'She's all yours, Jack. Do what you must with her, and I'll see you tomorrow.'

The bird of prey removed his top hat and opened his cloak of ribbed wings of steel, then laid himself down upon her with his mind lost in a red mist.

The doctor disappeared as he rode his bicycle as the "crow flies" back to Wimpole while the bird of prey savaged her flesh.

At Bedstead Square, Jack began to toss and turn inside his blankets as he sweated profusely. He was stuck inside his own nightmare and couldn't escape his frenzy, as Catherine Eddows lay upon the ground with her throat cut and her vital organs removed during her disembowelment.

'*I am here*,' he mumbled and spluttered. '*I am everywhere. I am a bird in the sky. I am everywhere.*'

And as his nightmare evolved he saw himself in a hospital theatre. This was his operation his mind told him, as he opened her up from her chest cavity to vagina, And as he continued to disembowel his mother, he could hear the deafening sound of people shouting his name whilst marching with their torches aflame, and their axes sharpened and at the ready to chop off his head.

'We must go. They are coming for us,' he could hear the voice of his doctor bouncing around inside his head, before he flew off towards the safety of this eyrie above the old greengrocers shop.

25

Now the doctor had been provided with the address of Pearly Poll, (aka) Mary Jane Kelly, he set about making himself familiar with the area of Spitalfields, as he and Thomas began frequenting the array of pubs set along Commercial Street and then Brick Lane. It wasn't long before they heard the sound of a soprano voice, when she began to sing an Irish folk song inside The Ten Bells drinking house, situated opposite Spitalfields Market. The tall, buxom redhead was a loud, brash figure of a woman, and she'd managed to turn the heads of both the doctor and Thomas as they stood at the bar with a glass of wine in hand.

'Now there's a jolly confident woman,' the doctor remarked under his breath as he scowled at her standing inside the doorway. They watched her as a tall white haired gentleman walked up to her and propositioned her by name.

'Mary Kelly, you have the voice of an angel,' he told her in a broad Scottish accent. She cackled wildly, before he took her by the hand and led her outside with her face illuminated, and her reward evident for all to see. She took the gentleman's arm and led him to her abode at Mitre Court, Dorset Street, just a stone's throw from the drinking house that was equal to a one minute walk.

The doctor and Thomas swiftly knocked back the rest of their wine and immediately followed them. They watched as she led him inside her room and closed the door shut behind her.

'There,' the doctor said. 'We have her. That's our pearly Poll.'

'I'm fairly sure he called her Mary,' Thomas replied.

'Yes, quite right, he did. But that's not her real name.

'Are you sure, old chap?'

'I'm positively sure. And I'd wager with you that her surname is Kelly.'

'Mary Kelly, then?'

'Yes. When they are hiding from the authorities, that's the assumed name they give themselves, as not to be distinguished one from another.'

'My God, you have been busy, haven't you?' Thomas replied respectfully.

***

The next morning the doctor conducted a private briefing at the greengrocers shop. He'd planned to interview three new prospective members for the society. A Bunsen burner flickered a dim flame as the group congregated around a small round table in anticipation of what commitment might be bestowed upon them on their journey to becoming fully signed up members.

In attendance, Montague John Druitt; a barrister from Dorset. He stood attentive, compliant and watchful as he listened to the doctor's speech concerning the reinvention of the old society and what must be achieved for them to sign up. Druitt wore a white silk scarf over the collar of his black cashmere coat; his hair waxed to create a neat centre parting, and along with his young dashing looks, he was the second son of medical practitioner William Druit.

Also in attendance was the Dorset architect, who'd succumbed to the idea of joining the society, after receiving the doctor's letter which had been endorsed by Thomas. The detective inspector was also in attendance and soon discovered that the doctor was doing the area of Whitechapel a huge service by putting the fear of God into the minds of the whores who walked the streets at night in search of their doss.

The doctor spoke excitedly about the future of all the Dorset men working in London, and how he intended to bring the first of them together, through one particular ceremony that would take place in the early hours at number 10 Mitre Court, Dorset Street. He told them just how they would have to prove their allegiance when they undertook the knife to spill the blood of the whore specifically chosen for the ceremony. And they quietly listened as he disclosed why he'd spilled the blood of Annie Chapman, and how it gave him an idea to save some her blood to use for his own initiation at the forthcoming ceremony. And the blood taken from Elizabeth Stride to secure Thomas's membership within the society.

'I have been working tirelessly to trace the whereabouts of this whore,' he told them. 'I got lucky when I stumbled across Catherine Eddows. She told me where I could find her.'

'So why this particular whore? What has she done, that she should be our sacrificial lamb?' the architect asked, with a worried gaze towards him.

'I thought I might be asked that question, so I can tell you, she is the whore who claimed that she witnessed a soldier from the Queen's Regiment murder a prostitute at Gunthorpe Alley back in August. I was instructed on behalf of Her Majesty's physician to find her, since the soldier involved is a close relative of the royal household. I have briefly spoken to the whore and she is definitely Pearly Poll, though she informed me that her name is Mary Jane Kelly, which I discovered is a pseudonym adopted by some of the prostitutes, as and when they're arrested for being drunk and disorderly. They never do reveal their true identities in fear of being sent to the clink. I have planned to meet with her tonight at her abode, and she is rather keen. Obviously she has no idea that she will be opened up by Monty here, when I let him loose on her. But I will remove her titties for him, so that she is comfortable in his hands.'

'Does her murder really have to be so brutal?' Druitt asked.

'Yes, I'm afraid it does. She has already embarrassed our Queen, and it will send a clear message to others thinking the same as she. I heard from a friend of mine at the Press Association that she is planning to sell her story before she disappears. I have it in good faith that she will board a boat for France, after she gets paid for her story. He also told me that she is familiar with Paris and is being seeked by the French authorities for theft of a trunk containing expensive garments. She stole the garments from a gentleman who she chaperoned while working as a prostitute in Knightsbridge. He has since offered a reward for the return of his wife's wardrobe.'

'So when are you planning this ceremony?' the architect asked in a gruff west country accent. Because I have to be back in Dorset by tomorrow evening. I have important meetings to attend before I return next weekend.'

'Well, then, we'll just have to wait for your return before we begin,' the doctor replied.

'Please do. I'll be sure to attend,' he remarked.

'So, are the rest of you good?' the doctor asked.

'On condition,' Montague John Driutt replied.

'And what's that, may I ask?'

'That I shan't have to get my hands sodden,' he said.

'You'll be just fine. I will bring with me everything required for the job in hand. Your hands will remain as clean as they are today.'

'Fine, then. Cannot wait.'

'Doctor, please don't make a mockery of the City of London Police. This will be hugely embarrassing for the Commissioner. There will be hell to pay when they discover her mutilated body,' the detective inspector reminded him.

'I know it will. But it will also send a message. You have my solemn word this will be the end. The ripping up will stop and we can all get on with promoting ourselves to London and making her the finest city in the world.'

'Fair enough,' the detective inspector replied.

'You will attend, I pray,' the doctor told him.

'Yes, but briefly,' the detective inspector replied.

'So, here's the plan; I will meet with her at precisely three a.m Sunday next. Once I'm inside her room, I will get to work immediately by silencing her. I shall prepare Monty for her full autopsy, that's after I give her over to my apprentice surgeon. I will bring with me a long spoon to sup her blood. Jack cannot, since he is not one of us, agreed?'

'Agreed,' they each replied, before they bowled their heads in unison and gave a one minute silence in respect of the whore's forthcoming death.

26

Switzerland

1923

At the chateau, the nurse poured water from a jug into a beaker as she stood by the doctor's right side and patted his head with a damp cloth. And as he lay dying, he stared at the panorama through the opened French doors. *I want to be cremated and have my ashes scattered in the gardens of my place of birth in Dorset.* The doctor thought within himself, before he turned his head to look up at the whitewashed ceiling. He thought back in retrospect when he was lecturing the medical students at Queen Mary's College, and a paragraph he had recited for them concerning the instant of death.

"Before the moment of death, the subjective astral body sometimes appears, emanating from the soul of the dying. For the act of death itself there is no mystery, we know precisely how death comes to pass. The mystery begins in the moment of death. The undiscovered country, the light that falls upon Elysian fields or happy hunting grounds or fills, which splendour the streets of an eternal city. When something like a white wave of the sea breaks o'er the brain and buries us in sleep."

And as he focused his eyes a vision appeared in front of him; the bird of prey hovering above his bed.

And as the nurse exited the room, the pastor entered and stood at the doctors right side, blocking his view of the lake. He stood silent whilst clutching a wooden crucifix in his right hand, his bible in tother. He began to mumble a prayer from his holy book when the doctor turned to him. 'Am I a good man, Father? Or am I a bad man?'

The pastor stared down at him and watched as the surgeon grimaced through all his pain. He could barely smile as the doctor tugged at his arm and aggressively pulled him closer with little strength he still had. He reiterated his question, but the pastor chose not to offer an opinion, instead a protracted silence came about while the pastor's puzzled counternounce embarrassed him as he stepped back and let the light shone down upon the dying man laid out in front of him.

The bird of prey moved into the light and spluttered his dismay at the pastor.

'He was a scholar.'

The door opened and the surgeon's wife entered, immediately followed by his editor, Charles Begwin.

The surgeon's wife was frail and wore her hair up into a neat little bun, which was grey in colour. Her tired brown eyes showed her pain and despair, because of her dying husband who she worshipped. While his editor was a large, sweaty, bullish man with a shaky but projective sounding voice. And he continuously wiped his brow with a handkerchief. He closed the door behind him, then began to follow her as she stepped towards the window and gazed out at the lake, glistening in the sunshine, and still like a heart that had stopped beating, but yet so full of life and enrichment that she could feel running through her veins.

'I need to have that manuscript. It's the best autobiography I have ever had the pleasure to read. Now where is it, Anne? What have you done with it?' He asked the back of her head, as she refused to even look at him while she continued to gaze at the lake and introspect.

'Look, Charles, I have told you once, if not twice, I burnt the damn thing. Why can you not believe me when I tell you that?' she finally turned to him and scorned.

'Oh, for heaven's sake. Those memoirs would have been read for many years to come. Your husband had much to say concerning his professional life in Whitechapel.'

'Those omissions would have caused every surgeon in the land huge embarrassment, legendary I think not,' she replied irksomely.

'If only you'd just given me the chance to publish them.' His face flushed, his clenched fist revealing to his utter torment, having read the full manuscript himself, but no longer had it in his grasp.

She showed him an ugly stare as she looked him in the eye He completely unaware of the sadness that lurked inside her very being, and the grief of losing her daughter to the same disease that was killing her husband; the irony, that he was an appendoctomist and had saved the king from certain death the day before his coronation.

'My husband lies dying of a perintinitis... yet all you can think about in his moment of sanctuary are a couple of chapters that I omitted from his book. We'll discuss it another time. Anyway, I thought you were supposed to be his dear friend. I want my husband to be remembered for all the good that he accomplished in his professional life. Christ! He deserves some gratitude at least, doesn't he?'

'Yes, but your husband wrote those memoirs for one reason, and one reason only… that was so it would be published! He did not write of his experiences just to inform the world of his sensational achievements either. There was real substance in those chapters. He wanted to set the record straight, to repent, and then leave this world with a clear conscience. He certainly won't be getting that privilege anymore, will he? And he even told me that himself, before he snatched it out of my hand.'

'Did he indeed?'

'Yes, he darn well did.'

'Well, I am very sorry. He didn't tell me. Anyway, he must have had some reservations if he did that to you.'

'If it hadn't been for that, I would have had that book bound and published and on sale in every book shop from here to John O'Groats.'

Well, as I say… it's too late now. I put it on the fire as I already told you.'

'Oh no, Anne!' he cried. 'Tell me you're lying, please…!'

'Oh don't despair. I've saved some of the chapters for you. For some reason beyond my reckoning, I decided that they can be published. Be grateful I've left you something at the very least, Charles.'

'Your husband was astonishing... The public has a right to know about his life. He lived… was two people at the very least. He's the most remarkable person I have certainly ever known.'

'Doctor Jekyll and Mr. Hyde, you mean? Now I am going to stay with my husband before he passes away. I still have a family to think about. Someday, I will be a grandmother and I would like my grandchildren to know that their grandfather was a decent man. And that's why I burnt the best part of his manuscript.'

'You really shouldn't have. If I had known that before, I wouldn't have travelled all the way to Geneva to ask for it.'

'No? I thought you were his friend.'

'I am his loyal and trusted editor, that's all.'

'Well I can see that now.' It's my good family name I have to protect from the likes of people like you, not entirely his. It is my family that will have had to live with the consequences of his book. And I couldn't allow my family that kind of bane, truthfully.'

'Oh well, then.'

'And if you print one false word about him, I will see to it that you never print another book again. Now good day. Let us be.'

'This is preposterous!'

'Is it? Take a close look at yourself for once.'

'You darn well know it, Anne!'

'Look, I am very sorry for you having to come all this way, but I cannot do anything about it now. I'll have the remaining chapters sent to your office when I get back.'

'Right. Goodbye to you, then.' He marched towards the door, then slammed it shut behind him upon his exit.

27

There was a cold chill in the air when Pearly Poll was out doing her usual pub crawl. Overcome with delirium that she was going to be handed a substantial sum, during the early hours from a man believed to be from the Press Association, she had packed a suitcase. But in fact, unbeknown to her, the man she would encounter would be her maker, which equated to her succumbing to her inevitable fate.

The doctor had instructed Montague John Druitt to chat her up and shill her whilst at The Ten Bells one evening. To pretend to be a reporter from a journal. His job was to set up a meeting with her to discuss her account of what actually occurred that unforgettable night back in early August concerning the death of Martha Tabram. But Pearly had arranged to vanish and to call upon a friend who'd resided in Knightsbridge Green. So upon securing a reward for her story she would travel back to the French capital and secure a place to stay, until such a time that she'd be forgotten by those who seeked to quieten her here in London.

Under the watchful eye of the bird of prey hovering above the Christ Church, she visited The Ten Bells where she sang to customers in turn for an alcoholic beverage, before selling herself for sex at her place betwixt the hours. And as the time grew closer for her meeting with the assumed journalist, she stumbled into the Brittania drinking house, situated at the corner of Dorset and Commercial. But little did Pearly know, she was being shadowed by her makers, Montagu John Druitt, Thomas, and the doctor. The job was to keep tabs on her whilst she solicited herself throughout the night and early hours. Thomas was the first to encounter her at the junction with Flower and Dean.

'Lend us a sixpence till later, will ya?' she asked, upon noticing he was a gentleman shabbily dressed; his garb, a long black coat and billycock hat. She noticed his blotchy skin colour as he stood casually smoking his clay pipe.

'I have nothing to give,' Thomas replied nonchalantly as she continued towards the Princess Alice at the junction with Wentworth, where she kept well oiled with the shillings she'd made from prostitution, before walking back to Millers Court.

Waiting for her was Joe Barnett. He'd turned up in a fury, because she was supposed to have met him at The Horn of Plenty but hadn't shown up.

'Where the 'ell 'av' you been?' he yelled at her as she stumbled inside the room and threw herself down on the bed. 'I've been lookin' for you. I say I've been lookin' everywhere for you. You were s'posed to bleedin' well meet me for a quicky at the 'orn,' he continued his rant towards her with a threatening gesture to clump her, but instead smashed her window with his bare fist.

'What'd ya go and do that for?' she yelled at him. 'Now I'll have to get it fixed. And you can pay me for it, that's what.'

'Don't take the piss outta me, Mary. Standing there like a lemon waitin' for ya.'

'Oh go away, Joey,' she cried. 'Leave us alone wontcha? I've gotta meet a gentleman here later, so I ain't got no time for ya tonite. Come back t'mmora and we'll have a drink, then, I promise ya, I will.'

'You better bleedin' 'ad, I tell ya, you bleedin' better 'ad, he barked as he stormed off and left her sitting on the bed.

As Joe Barnett stormed off into the night it began to rain. Pearly climbed off the bed and put on some make-up, before she brushed her long red hair as she hummed a tune to herself. Upon leaving her room she decided to take a stroll along Commercial Street where the doctor waited at the corner with Thrawl. His eyes followed her as she headed towards him. He passed her a mischievous grin, his hands placed down by his side as he held on to a pair of kid gloves, and a large brown parcel containing all the surgical equipment required to complete the job. When she confronted him, he placed a hand lightly upon her shoulder.

'Ullo. I can tell what you want,' she implied.

'Let's go,' he told her.

'You wanna go to my place, do ya?' she replied. 'It's only across the road.'

'As long as we're not disturbed,' he replied knowingly.

'Oh, you'll be alright. I'll make you feel quite comfortable,' she said, before she took his arm in hers and guided him to Millers Court.

'I do hope so,' he replied. 'You're just the sort of lady I've been looking for.'

'Well, as long as you pay me generously, you won't be disappointed.'

'Is that so?'

'Oh yes.'

Upon reaching her room, she led him inside, then quietly closed the door shut. He stood over her as she sat herself down on the bed and leant forward to take off her boots. The doctor was dressed in his finest attire, consisting of a black felt hat and an astrakhan coat with a thick gold chain that housed the red seal of the Royal College of Surgeons. This doctor was no ordinary doctor, he was a surgeon and was next in line for the top job at the ducal palaces, should he complete his mission of silencing Pearly Poll.

He could barely contain his excitement as he glanced behind and noticed the window pane smashed, so he placed his parcel in front of the hole to stop a person spying. He quickly slipped out of his coat and took off his hat, then placed them on the hook at the back of the door.

'Come here,' she said as she looked up at him and beckoned him towards her. 'We'll have to make it quick, cos I've gotta get ready for a very important person and he'll be here soon.'

'All right,' he replied as he towered over her.

And as she laid down upon the crumpled bed, she opened her thighs for him. But he viciously grabbed her tiny throat before she could utter a sound. Her eyes bulged before him as he choked her half to death, then sliced her throat from east to west, as she stared up at him in abject shock and horror. Pearly hadn't time to react as her blood seeped quickly from her deep wound and covered his hand. Upon her execution he checked his timepiece then opened his parcel filled with surgical wear.

And as he prepared his tools for the initiation ceremony, he rolled up his shirt sleeves and tied an apron around his waist.

And when the clock struck the hour at 3 am, the doctor opened the door for the Dorset men.

'Let's get this over with,' Druitt immediately uttered in trepidation upon his entry.

'First, I should make her comfortable for you, but Thomas you should keep watch. 'Do not let anyone pass,' he told him as he walked over to the bed and cut away at her clothes, before he removed her breasts and placed one behind her head and the other under her foot. 'There. She awaits your expertise, M,J. D.'

Druitt grabbed the knife from the doctor's grasp and like a man possessed by evil, began by ferociously stabbing and cutting into her flesh like it was a piece of rotten meat. And as Druitt continued to besiege her like a rabid dog they stood quietly and watched as Thomas kept watch outside.

And when there was no more to be done, Jack was let loose on her, in his mind a bird of prey, ripping and digging his blunt knife into her like a prehistoric beast from another world.

'Men, our work here is done,' the doctor said. 'Let me raise a toast to our new beginning, and all the Dorset men here in London. Our Job of finding and silencing Pearly Poll has been achieved,' he said, before they each supped her blood with a wooden spoon.

28

Upon reaching his flat in the west of London, Druitt immediately opened a bottle of scotch and poured it down his throat as though it was cider. He violently shook his head upon reflection of his evil deed upon the sacrificial whore. The trauma suffered, because of his deliberate act to become a member of the reinvented medieval society, had overwhelmed him to such a degree that he soon began to vomit into the toilet basin. His total despair, due to his participation, threw his mind into absolute chaos; a frenzy of anxiety as he banged his head hard on the rim of the toilet bowl, causing an abrasion from which he couldn't recover. This depressive desperation that he'd inherited from his mother was too much for him to bear as he considered his fate. The embarrassment caused by his homosexuality and promiscuity among the students at Blackheath College had caused his reputation as a barrister to become untennable, all because of the people who had delved into his personal affairs and passed judgement upon him. This dire existence had finally taken its toll, and along with the bloody dissection of the whore, M.J Druitt made up his mind to take his ghastly secret with him to the depths of London's mighty heart; the River Thames.

So he climbed to his feet and threw on his coat, before he stormed out of the flat in haste. And upon reaching the Hammersmith Bridge, he stood and gazed in reverie down at the river swirling wildly beneath his feet, calling him and causing his head to spin out of control. And with his mind lost inside a vortex, he stomped down the dozen steps to the banks of the river where he gazed into the blackness and howling wind that only encouraged further into its path. And with the angry splashes of water covering his feet he looked up at the iron bridge, for not a soul, nor creature to witness the augury of death about to be befall him. This once spritely young sportsman who'd been born into a well-to-do family had finally acquiesced to his inevitable fate, simply because he could carry no longer that burden of weight which equated to his depravity and humiliation. He fell down upon his knees and loaded his pockets with the heaviest of stones that he could feel within the slimy sludge as he stumbled into the freezing cold water. And with his tormented fractured mind fixed without persuasion upon drowning himself, the downpour of rain began to fall upon him and assist him further towards his anonymity.

'I'm so sorry, Mother. Please forgive me,' he looked up at the moon and cried. 'I cannot suffer in this world of hatred any longer. It is time for me to end my life.' Montague John Druitt dragged himself into the deep blackness of the river, then sank towards the streambed, only for a thin sphere of air to remember him by.

29

With the suicide of M.J Druitt and Thomas's return to Dorset, the doctor decided to concentrate his efforts on his workload, while his patient had been sent away to convelesce in Northamptionshire. The doctor had sent him to stay with friends of his. He'd had fits when he heard that Jack had been asked to frighten his friend's two adolescent daughters. And he knew the fresh air would do his patient's lungs the world of good.

The authorities were at sixes-and-sevens in regards to catching the culprit, as they clutched at straws to naming the killer of Mary Jane Kelly at Millers Court, but the doctor was sure she had been Pearly Poll all along. The police commissioner had resigned, and the detective inspector was taken off the case and sent back to Scotland Yard, Whitehall.

By this time, the nature of the murders had ceased and it was assumed by those in command that the Ripper had ended his murder spree with the last whore. They were positively sure there would not possibly be another murder that could exceed that of Millers Court. Upon examination of her cadaver, it was mentioned that the women's corpse had suffered a full dissection and removal of body parts, and that only a mortuary technician could have inflicted such a savage surgical attack upon a living soul.

However, upon Jack's return to Bedstead Square his nightmares had worsened, and like a magnet drawn found himself visiting the old greengrocers shop more often than not. The difficulty was that he hadn't still been able to distinguish fantasy from reality. Haunted, bitter and tormented, he continued to be a bird of prey, and this fact had given the doctor a huge dilemma. His patient's disease had also worsened and begun to take its toll upon him as his decline became evident for all to see. It was following a savage attack upon a whore known locally as Clay Pipe Annie inside an alleyway close to the greengrocers shop, the doctor suspected his patient to be the perpetrator, since it was reported that her attacker had been physically impaired and almost too weak to carry out his attack upon her. She had suffered a devastating attack with her throat and abdomen cut. And when the doctor heard about this, he became furious, so he immediately marched over to Bedstead Square to speak to Jack concerning this matter, as he knew the injuries inflicted upon her bore all the hallmarks of his patient's *modus operandi;*

But on this occasion, Jack was asleep and lying upon his plumped up pillows, snoring and purring like a sleeping lion. In his mind he was flying high above the clouds and tipping his hat to all those that peered up at him, waving at him as he dropped giant blackberries to cover them in that thick red goo. For the first time in his life Jack was in his element as he fantasised and succumbed to his pending death.

The doctor opened the door and noticed Jack was sleeping, but gritted his teeth and quietly stepped over to his bed.

'I'm sorry, Jack, but I did warn you what would happen if you continued to disobey me.' the doctor whispered into his ear. ' I love you, Jack. Goodbye,' he said to him as he gently slid one hand beneath his pillow, then with his other hand, with one short, sharp twist Jack's neck snapped, along with his everlasting nightmare scenario as he fell to the ground at lightning speed and exploded upon impact, leaving a thick red goo in his wake. The doctor leant over his cadaver and softly kissed the top of his head, before he sat himself down on the bed and gently stroked him while a single tear began to roll down his cheek. He took out a handkerchief from his top pocket and blew hard his nose. And after some time spent sitting there, staring down with affection at his patient he gathered himself and quietly left the room. It was the end of a beautiful relationship for him personally. But the doctor simply had to withdraw and not let his patient jeopardise his personal kudos. There was a new life waiting for the chief surgeon at the London Hospital. Sir. William Gull was about to retire, due to illness, and the ducal palaces were expecting a new house surgeon. The doctor had paid his dues to them and earned their respect for him, since Sir. William Gull had sanctioned his credentials for services rendered.

Epilogue

Switzerland

1923

There was a protracted silence, palpable inside the dimly lit room as the old surgeon closed his eyes for the last time. His wife stood beside him as she held his hand. The pastor continued to mumble coherently as he read out his last rights, whilst the apparition stood aimlessly at the bottom of his bed. With the French doors wide open and the sun disappearing over the horizon the old surgeon's eyes suddenly opened wide. His wife shuddered and stepped back afeard of the occurrence of death as she bowed her head and joined in a prayer for him.

'He has gone, hasn't he?' she uttered as she looked up at the pastor.

He nodded his head to certify the surgeon's passing.

'He lived his life and did what he wanted,' she remarked passively. 'He gave to our country all he had to give. I think he will never be forgotten, I'm sure of that.'

The door opened and Christopher, the surgeon's brother, quietly stepped inside the room.

'I'm so sorry. Am I too late? Has he lamented?' he asked with his cap in hand.

'Yes, he has,' his wife replied, before she put her handkerchief to her eyes and sobbed.

And as a burst of light lit up the room, the face of the Elephant Man morphed into the bird of prey as he opened his cape with ribbed wings of steel knives and leapt through the open doors. The surgeon's wife felt a chill, before she turned and closed the doors shut with a knowing look upon her face.

The End.

Printed in Great Britain
by Amazon